Copyright © 2020 by Mara Webb

All rights reserved. No part of this publication may be reproduced, distributed, or transmitted in any form or by any means, including photocopying, recording, or other electronic or mechanical methods, without the prior written permission of the publisher, except in the case of brief quotations embodied in critical reviews and certain other noncommercial uses permitted by copyright law.

PRIMROSE & POISON: A WITCH COZY MYSTERY

RAVEN BAY MYSTERIES BOOK 1

MARA WEBB

I closed my eyes and made a wish. I fantasized that I was surrounded by loved ones singing happy birthday and that I would open my eyes to be handed piles of gifts. When I looked again, I was still sitting in a diner by a gas station in the middle of nowhere. There was no candle to blow out on the plastic wrapped muffin I had just been handed either.

"Refill?" the waitress asked. I gratefully nudged my mug towards her as she poured hot coffee and then pulled it back across the counter towards myself. I was less than an hour away from my destination, but the light had flashed up on the dash to tell me I needed to fill up the tank, so I figured I would throw myself a little pity party while I was here.

The car was filled with all my earthly possessions, I'd left my dignity back in my old apartment. I was moving back to my hometown and there was nothing exciting about it, other than spending some time with my mom. As I would be living with her though, I was sure the novelty would wear off quickly.

I stared down at the printout that I had brought with me from the car. It was a checklist of things to do when you move from one state to another. I would have to forward my mail, get a new physician, transfer my driver's license…urgh. I folded up the sheet, settled my bill and walked out into the sunlight.

I looked over at my rental car, filled with boxes of clothes, files from my old job and the comforter from my bed. Turned out I didn't own much. I had thought packing everything would have taken longer but I had been renting a furnished apartment and leaving my life behind had taken less than an hour.

I had been working as an investigator for a newspaper, it had been everything I had wanted since I graduated high school and it had been so fulfilling to solve mysteries with the rest of my team. There were a few of us in my department and we looked into all sorts of criminal activity, but we'd missed something big.

The owner of the paper had started changing some numbers around on the company accounts, hoping he could take a few thousand dollars for himself here and there and no one would notice. He got carried away and got caught. Our newspaper was sold off to a competitor and we were all fired on the spot.

I had only just been able to make rent every month, so I hadn't put a single penny aside for a rainy day. That meant that I was moving back in with my mother, on my birthday, and I had the weight of uncertainty hanging over me.

Happy Birthday to me…

Back in the car I began to recognize the landscape and could see the lake in the distance. I leaned forward to switch off my GPS as I could use my memory to take me the rest of the way. You can take the girl out of Raven Bay, but you can't take Raven Bay out of the girl.

By the time I actually pulled into town it was mid-afternoon. I wondered if I should head straight to my mom's place or walk about the town first. It seemed risky to park the car on the main road with all my stuff inside, what if someone broke in through the window and took everything? I laughed to myself because I was still stuck in the 'big city' mentality of crime and mistrust of your fellow citizen, those things didn't happen here.

On one side of the road was an endless canopy of Douglas Firs coating the hills, on the other was the beginnings of the town I had grown up in. I slowed the car down and as the trees began to thin out, the sidewalks began to grow more populated. Soon I was looking at the familiar buildings of my childhood and it felt like maybe life here wouldn't be so bad after all.

I spotted the bakery that my mom used to take me to on weekends and turned to pull up in the parking lot behind it. My mom had *probably* remembered that it was my birthday today, but I thought I should buy myself a cake and take it to her place. We could always eat it tomorrow if she was baking me one herself.

I searched my memory for images of the outside, I was trying to figure out if they had updated the place since I was away, but it looked exactly the same. It almost looked like a giant red barn, a regular sized white door in the center was framed by two large windows either side. Small trees lined the short path from the sidewalk and were planted inside stubby log chunks, giving it a fall aesthetic all year round.

A square sign above the door read, 'Autumn's Woodland Bakery', and I smiled at the thought of every huckleberry scone I had shared with my mom in this place. I pushed open the door and a silence fell over the people inside. A few faces looked familiar, but they were eyeing up the strange woman that had just walked through the door.

The layout inside hadn't changed much either, it looked like the chairs had been upgraded but the timber-top tables were the same. If I looked hard enough, I bet I could find the one I had carved my name into with my friends one day after a math exam that had gone badly.

"Welcome to Autumn's, you look new so come this way," a friendly girl said. When she turned to walk away from me, I saw that her brown hair was braided down to her waist. Her uniform consisted of a dusty orange polo shirt and black shorts, nothing much had changed in here. She gestured towards a stool at the counter and I perched myself on top.

She smiled at me and her hazel eyes sparkled beneath dramatic false lashes. She had delicate features that seemed familiar, but I was having trouble placing her in my memory.

"My mom will help you choose something delicious," she said, spinning away to deal with another customer. *Her mom?*

"Astrid!" a woman shrieked. "Is it really you?" Before I knew it, a pair of arms were wrapped around my body like a boa constrictor and I felt the air being squeezed out of me.

"Yes...yes, it is," I struggled. The arms released me and the body they were attached to ran around so that I could see who it was. Autumn, the owner of the bakery, was beaming at me with glistening eyes and she didn't seem to have aged a day. Her shouting my name seemed to have helped the customers that were trying to figure out who I was, and a small round of applause broke out to celebrate my return. I blushed aggressively.

"I heard you were coming back, but I couldn't bring myself to believe it until I saw you in the flesh. How are you?" Autumn rested her hand on my right shoulder as she waited for my response. If she had heard that I was moving back to Raven Bay, then she probably had also heard the reasons why, it was a look of pity.

"I'm good," I lied.

"Oh honey," she cooed, stroking my face gently before leap frogging over her counter like a teenage gymnast. "Let's get you an orange roll." She began to move with the speed I remembered from years ago, it was like she had a thousand arms. In seconds she had produced a small white plate, reached into the glass display to pull out a roll and the coffee machine was grinding beans.

"How did you remember that these are my favorite?" I smiled. The scent was heavenly, and I felt my mood instantly lift.

"I couldn't possibly reveal my secrets," she winked. "Your mom must be over the moon that you are home."

I watched Autumn turn her back as she prepared my drink and then placed a huge Caffe mocha down in front of me. I didn't start drinking coffee until I moved to the city, but this had become my go-to order, how could she have known that? I looked at her face questioningly, but she just winked again and waited for me to speak.

"My mom? Oh yeah, I haven't seen her yet. I couldn't resist coming in here first," I grinned, taking another bite of my roll.

"Attie, your mother will be beside herself waiting for you to show up!" She was using the nickname that I had left behind when I left town, I hadn't heard anyone call me that in years.

"I'm going straight there after this!" I spluttered through a mouthful of food. I was defensive in the same way you are when a teacher catches you doing something you shouldn't. We had fallen back into our old dynamic and I felt comforted by it. I heard the bell above the door ring and turned to see who had entered.

"Who is parked out back with the busted taillight?" the man boomed. I raised my hand nervously and the police officer approached. I had backed into a wall at some point during my journey here and had forgotten all about it. I didn't want to know what the rental company was going to charge me to fix it.

"Listen here, Evan. Astrid has had a very long drive to get here and I won't have you coming in acting like a tough guy over a bit of shattered plastic. Watch your mouth!" Autumn commanded. She was thrusting a cloth in his direction as she spoke, and I looked back at his face.

"Yes, I mean, obviously I wasn't going to..." he spluttered. His demeanor softened and I felt a smile grow across my face. Autumn was in charge of everybody once they stepped into her bakery, she was like everyone's mother and no one disrespected her.

"You either sit and eat, or go fix it for her," Autumn insisted.

"I'll eat first," Evan mumbled. He slid onto the stool at the end of the row, putting a few feet of air between us. He looked over at me and we locked eyes for a few seconds in silence. "Astrid? Is that what Autumn just said?"

"Yeah," I replied. "You're not Evan *Brooks* by any chance?"

His eyes lit up and a huge smile spread across his face. Oh, his glorious, handsome face. He had gone to my high school and was one of the hottest guys around, every single one of us had a crush on Evan Brooks. Those baby blues had lost none of their charm.

"Oh my goodness, Attie! Oh, your mom has been telling everybody about your return, she must be over the moon!" he smiled. Gee, everyone was sure convinced that my mom was thrilled about my sorry return. They were all using the same turn of phrase too, it was funny really. I parted my lips to speak but was cut off.

"It's her birthday you know," Autumn announced. Had she really remembered the date after all these years? "So really I think you should fix up that taillight as a gift and leave her be."

"I can do that, if you give me a little bit of time to sort it out, I can fix it right up. Good as new! I'm good with cars," he grinned. Those eyes were sending me back to high school geography class in an instant, tapping him on the shoulder to ask him questions I already had the answer to just so he would look at me.

"Sure? I can leave it. I'll walk to my mom's shop from here," I replied.

"I could give you a ride," Evan offered. I felt my face heat up.

"I've been driving for hours, it would be good to stretch my legs," I said, and looked back at Autumn. "Could I get a large funfetti cake to go? This one here?" I asked, pointing through the glass counter.

Autumn smiled knowingly as if she had anticipated the question. She slid the glass door aside and began to box it up.

I thought about whether I had mentioned that it was my birthday or not, I felt sure that I hadn't. Maybe my mom had gone around telling everybody about *that,* too. Evan had taken off his police officer's hat and placed it down on the counter as Autumn handed him a plate of hot food. She really was like a second mother to all of us.

I reached into my purse to dig around for the money I would need to settle the bill, but Autumn reached over to place her hand on my arm.

"It's on me sweetheart, you're part of the family again now," she smiled. She winked again and I wondered if there had been this much winking during my last visit or if this was a new thing she was trying out. Evan said he would drop by my mom's store and get the car back to me once he was done with it. I was giddy at the thought of seeing him again despite still staring at his face.

All I had to do now was go to my mom's little flower shop and face the music. I was nervous and excited equally, and for good reason.

2

The weather made for a pleasant walk from the bakery. I wasn't entirely sure where I was going as mom opened her flower shop after I left town, and I hadn't been back here in years. I was always making excuses about being too busy with work, I was lucky she was even still speaking to me. I mean, we spoke on the phone all the time, I just never drove here.

Mom had visited my apartment a bunch of times, she was definitely putting in more effort with our relationship than I was. I had been so career focused that I was neglecting the things that I should be nurturing. She had given me some brief directions for how to get to her flower shop and soon I was standing in front of, 'The Twisted Tulip'.

It sounded more like a Halloween store than a sweet place to buy roses and lilies. I had heard her talking about a huge demand for the things she was selling and had brushed it off as her being overly enthusiastic, but the building was much bigger than I had expected.

It was situated at a junction in the road that meant you could drive past it on two sides. I couldn't remember if this building had been something else, or if it had always sold plants. It was old brick with forest green windows, the metal frame of the glass awning painted to match. It was three stories high and the vines that were wrapped around it made it look like it had been around forever.

Walking inside I was met with a wall of scent from every flower in the place. There was a hint of compost in the mix too, and maybe some burning incense. I had never seen so much plant life in one place before, it was beautiful, and I considered that maybe mom had been right about the demand. She had been running the place for a few years now, I imagined people would be willing to drive here from out of town.

"Hey there, how can I help?" a squeaky voice asked. I looked around for the person that had made the noise, but I couldn't see a soul in here anywhere, maybe they were hiding behind a palm tree or something. "I'm down here!"

I looked down to see an elderly woman with cropped orange hair and large tortoise shell glasses. They were like two giant circles that magnified her eyes and eyebrows giving her an unusual aesthetic. She was shorter than me but was carrying a potted plant that had been hiding her like a camouflaged soldier.

"Hi, I'm looking for my mom. Aster? She told me to meet her here," I stuttered.

"You must be Astrid, take a seat kiddo! I'm Cherry, I work here with your mother and there isn't a darn thing to know about plants that isn't kept up here," she said, tapping her head. "You're going to be learning from me mostly I bet!"

"I haven't actually decided what I'm going to be doing now that I'm back. I thought I might see if there were any vacancies at the paper," I said. My mom had mentioned something about working in the store, but I wouldn't have a clue where to start with these things and it wasn't a passion of mine. I was glad my mom was enjoying it, but I just didn't see myself selling herbs to home cooks.

"You'll be here, you can do other things too. You can have more than one dream, sweet cheeks," Cherry mumbled as she disappeared behind a row of house plants. I quickly got the impression she had the same sort of authority that Autumn held in her bakery, they were each queens of their realm and I was floating around between them, doing what I was told.

There was a stool beside the counter, and I jumped up onto it and wondered if I should call my mom or just wait. I hadn't told her what time I would be arriving, I figured she would just be at work so it wouldn't matter.

"Excuse me, do you have any blue roses?" a quivering voice asked. I turned expecting to see a frail woman waiting behind me but was shocked to see a cheerleader in full uniform.

"I... I don't actually work here, not really," I replied, stunned by the sight. It had been the same uniform that had been worn at the town high school when I was a student, surely it had been modernized over the years. I couldn't believe they would still be wearing it, I stood staring at her as if I knew her somehow. She was a teenager though; I must be confused by her clothing.

"Oh, well could you let me know if you find any?" she asked. I heard a rustle coming from the row of house plants and Cherry reappeared.

"Cherry, do we have any blue roses?" I asked. She stopped dead in her tracks and looked up at me with her huge magnified eyes. Her arms dropped to her side as she contemplated what to say to me, she looked exasperated as if I had just asked to borrow a thousand dollars.

"What on earth would *you* need blue roses for?" she finally said.

"They aren't for me, they're for..." I turned to point at the cheer-leader, but she was gone. "There was a girl here, she...huh. She must be here somewhere." I stood up from the stool and looked around, unsure where to look first. The shop was a maze of flowers.

"Young thing? Cheerleader? Sad look in her eye?" Cherry asked. I nodded. "Oh... and you can see her? Very interesting!" Cherry's magnified eyes blinked a few times behind her giant tortoiseshell glasses. "Ignore her! I mean, great news for you *obviously*, but don't worry about that for now. You should dip your toe in, don't jump in with both feet!"

"...What?" I had no idea what she was talking about, maybe the incense wafting through this shop had melted her brain. It had been so strong when I walked in, but I had quickly become accustomed to it and couldn't smell it anymore.

"I had a quick look for your mother upstairs, she could be anywhere," Cherry said as she bit a chunk out of some jerky she was holding. "Want a bite?"

"I'm uh… good, thanks," I replied. She shrugged and took another bite. "How long have you worked with my mom?"

"Oh, a long time. I don't keep track of these things really. I remember you when you were a little girl, running about with that hair like a dusty sunset, giddy thing you were too. Always smiling for some reason," she laughed.

My ginger locks had been a horrid thing to have as a child, the older I had gotten, the happier I was to stand out. "Always smiling? Was I?" I asked. "I don't remember that."

I didn't even remember Cherry for that matter.

"I lived in that house on the hill that you all used to play 'knock and run' on, you used to scream *watch out for the snake lady* and throw eggs," she said, taking another drink.

"Huh? Oh, I remember being scared of a snake lady, I never threw eggs or knocked on your door. I was terrified of that house; I never would have dared. It was you the whole time?" I couldn't believe it. There had been all sorts of crazy rumors about that old house and the wicked woman living inside, Cherry seemed reasonably normal.

"I bet your mother kept you on the straight and narrow, eh? I'll make a few calls, see if I can track her down for you. Oh, and happy birthday by the way. Are you sure you don't want some jerky?" she asked as she went to disappear somewhere in the back again.

"I'm fine without," I said, wondering how *everyone* seemed to know that it was my birthday. Cherry slipped out of sight and I stood up with the intention of browsing the store.

"Did she tell you where they are?"

I whipped my head around to see the cheerleader standing there once again. I jumped in surprise, tripped over my own shoe and stumbled backwards. She reached out a hand to stop me falling and I tried to grab it, but my fingers passed straight through her wrist.

I fell back and knocked over a bucket of sunflowers.

How did I miss? I thought I had seen my hand glide *through* her arm, but that couldn't be right. The stupid incense must be getting to me. It had been a very stressful week and I was clearly feeling the effects of it all.

"...What just happened?" I said, staring at my own hand in confusion and disbelief.

"I just forget, sorry," the cheerleader replied. "Even after all this time! It's just nice to speak to someone though, not many people can do that. You must be special."

"I don't understand," I said, clambering up from the ground and returning the flowers to the bucket.

"Attie! There you are!" My mom ran at me with her arms open wide and smothered me in a great big hug. As she did, I looked up and thought I saw the cheerleader disappear into thin air.

I clearly needed sleep.

"Hey mom, I made it," I smiled. She was hugging me so tight that I couldn't wriggle free, finally she loosened her grip to look at me.

"Happy birthday! I didn't forget, I bet you thought I would, but I didn't! I'm throwing you a big party at Fives, and everyone is coming, there will be cake and music! Isn't that great?" she said, bouncing up and down on the spot with delight. I hadn't been to Fives in a *long* time. It was the main bar in town.

"Sounds awesome." I wasn't sure if that was a lie or not, I didn't know who she was referring to when she said 'everyone' was coming. Any friends I had here must be long gone, right? I couldn't imagine that many of my old gang would have stuck around when they could go off to explore the big wide world. Although Evan had stayed...who knows?

"Attie has been talking to *the* cheerleader," Cherry chimed in.

"Really?! What did she say?" my mom asked, a hand on each of my shoulders and a serious expression on her face.

"She was asking about blue roses, why? Is she a thief?!" I replied. They both seemed so bothered that I had interreacted with this girl, was she banned from the store or something?

"Blue roses?" Mom said to Cherry in a hushed tone. "That's new..." She turned back to face me. "Well it's amazing that you can see her. We needed someone around here with enough ability to sort that one out."

"What do you mean?" I said, confused.

"If you had a conversation with her, then you can see *and* hear her. Most of the people in town don't know she is here at all; the others can hear her occasionally. You can do it all! You came of age but got out of town before you settled into your powers, now that you are home again, they are getting all fired up," Mom grinned.

"Your family has been given many gifts and you seem to have developed a great one, Attie. With a witch like you in town, things are looking up!" Cherry laughed.

Wait. A *what?!*

3

"*I* was going to ease her in a bit more gently than that," my mom said to Cherry.

"It's done now though, isn't it?!" Cherry said, trying to fake a look of remorse that nobody was buying. "You should have told her years ago!" Cherry shoved a glass of water into my hand.

"Told me what? I don't understand what just happened with that girl in here and you said something about a witch?" I stammered. I was struggling to piece together the words because my brain was foggy with exhaustion, somehow a sip of the drink Cherry had given me helped bring some clarity.

"Sweetheart," my mom began. "Sweet baby doll, my little angel..."

"Get to the point," I interrupted.

"That girl you saw is not alive anymore. She probably looks totally normal to you, not weird and floaty like you might expect."

"Wait, are you trying to tell me she is a ghost?" I chuckled. "Gee, I should definitely get some sleep because this is not a great time to pull a prank on me. I don't know up from down, mom. I've been back in town for five minutes; I need an adjustment period."

"Listen up sweet cheeks," Cherry said sternly. "You saw a ghost. It's a rare treat to have 'the sight' and you are going to probably have plenty of odd encounters because of it. If that ghost goes around telling the others we have a witch with ghost sight here, then you will be bombarded!"

"Why do you keep saying witch?" I asked, my brow crinkled together as I watched the two women in front of me sigh with frustration. I didn't know what they were trying to tell me but the both seemed annoyed that I was missing the point.

"Astrid," mom said. "You are a witch. I am a witch. Cherry is a witch. See that woman over there?" She pointed at a blonde lady that was rubbing the leaves of a sharp looking plant in the far corner, she saluted in acknowledgment of us. "She's a witch too. You left before you really came into your powers, but now that you are home, they are booting up in double quick time."

"Girl come on. This can't be a total surprise to you!" Cherry smirked. "Haven't you seen some weird things in your time? Maybe as a child?"

Plenty of weird things *had* happened but I had always brushed them off. I had walked into my empty house after school several times feeling hungry, only to wander into the kitchen and find a full roast dinner and a fresh batch of cookies waiting on the table. I had dreamt that I had redecorated my room, then woken up to find that the walls had changed color and I had new furniture, I thought I was a sleep-decorator or something.

"This is all a bit much to take in," I said as I looked around for a chair. I found one and sat down quickly.

"It is going to take a bit of getting used to, honey," mom said. "But we can catch you up to speed on everything! I'll start here. This isn't just a flower shop! We sell ingredients for spells. Potions, brews, concoctions...whatever you want to call them. If you need it, we sell it. There is a basement for our *special* gatherings with the town witches, we will do a big welcome for you at the next meeting. But for now, have this."

She handed me a printout of the things to do when you move to a new state, it was similar to the list I had brought with me, only she had changed a few things.

"I made you an appointment to see the physician, I figured you would have a lot of stress about this and at the moment you would think that the best way to sort that out is with *medicine* and *science*," she laughed, making dramatic air quotes with her fingers. "Soon you'll come around to our way, but I figured you'd like a doctor until then."

"I was thinking I might get some shut eye—"

"Listen sweetie, mommy has some special surprises that she needs to plan. So it would be a *real* big favor if you were busy for thirty minutes! This doctor's appointment is the perfect opportunity!"

"Just wander over now!" Cherry said. "It's usually quiet in the afternoon. Heck, all of the time actually…"

I realized quickly that I didn't have much of a say in this matter. It sounded like my mom had gone to some effort to plan a party for me, and I didn't want to throw that in her face.

"Okay, I guess I'll… go to the doctors," I said.

"That's the spirit!" she chirped. "After this it's all party!" Mom helped me onto my feet, and I could feel my pulse racing. I needed sleep. I needed to soak my body in a hot bath and then crawl into a bed to lie perfectly still for 12 to 15 hours, then I'd be back to normal. "Go and see Dr. Bailey, then you can tick this off your little list here and feel good about it. I know you like lists," mom whispered. "It's right out the doors then straight down, a cute little—"

"I think I remember," I said. Mom smiled.

"I'll call you in a bit!" she shouted as I made for the entrance. I gestured that I was leaving and stepped out of the front door. The sunlight on my face felt refreshing and I took a deep breath of the fresh air that was in plentiful supply in the lake side town. It was so quiet everywhere that I was struggling to understand why I had moved away in the first place. As a fresh high school graduate, I hadn't wanted quiet. I had wanted action, noise, people.

Things had changed.

I walked up the street in the direction of the building for the town physician's office. The flower shop was somewhat isolated from other businesses, but in less than two minutes I was right in the center of the town. A row of buildings either side of the road was what passed for a town center here.

I spotted the sign for 'Healthcare on the Bay' and confidently stepped through the door. It was nestled in between a Chinese restaurant and a shoe store. It had a strong smell of disinfectant. The woman sitting at reception had her head in a magazine and didn't notice me enter. I coughed gently to try and get her attention and she nearly fell out of her chair.

"Ah!" she screamed. "Huh? Hey? What?!?" she flustered, pulling herself back onto her seat. "Oh! Hello! How can I help? Do you have an appointment?"

"Someone's here?!" a voice shouted from another room. I hadn't said a word yet, but my presence seemed to have triggered a lot of panicked activity from the staff. A doctor stuck his head out of a side room and his face lit up when he saw me.

"Are you here to register with us?" he said, flashing every tooth in a giant smile.

"Yeah, is that cool with you guys? …You all seem a bit on edge!" I chuckled nervously.

"We don't get a lot of new sign ups; we actually haven't had a patient in since last week! It's a quiet town," the receptionist smiled. She looked slightly younger than my mom, but that was hard to use as a reference point as my mom didn't seem to age at the same speed as other people.

"Come on in," the doctor said, using a beckoning motion with his hands to speed me along. I found myself almost running across the tiles to get to his door even though there was no need to rush. I was getting swept up in their excitement. "Let me see, I think I had a call saying someone was coming. Could you state your full name for me?"

"Astrid Atwood," I replied. I lowered myself onto the chair beside his desk and sat up very straight as if my posture was being graded.

"Attie?" he said, looking away from his computer screen. "Attie, it's me! It's Dax! We had anatomy together, do you remember?"

I studied his face and tried to picture it without the peach-fuzz beard. He didn't look like the type of doctor I was used to; his facial hair hadn't been trimmed in a few days and his short, auburn curls were untamed. He was completely unfamiliar.

"Uh, yeah, yeah I think so!" I lied. "Sorry, it's been a really long time since then and I am crazy tired. It's been a weird day." I didn't want to tell him about the witch stuff, that would be a sure-fire way to get a mental health assessment that would delay my bedtime even further.

"I'm having a tough week myself," he said. It's so good to see a familiar face," he smiled. As he did, I vaguely began to recognize his dimples and memories of science class together, then all at once my memory of him clicked back into place, as though some distant part of my brain had just woken up.

"Dax!" I said out loud, stating his name to myself as I finally placed him. "I do remember you! Hey, anatomy class obviously paid off for you, a doctor! That's great. Your dad must be proud," I said, remembering that his parents were the pushy type. They wanted him to excel and limited his social life because of it.

"Yeah, he's really uh…" he mumbled. "Say! What do you do now?"

"Well I'm a—look, I've been getting this pain in my shoulder after I exercise," I said, desperately hoping he would not make me tell him that my life had fallen apart and I was living with my mom who was convinced she had magic powers.

Thankfully, Dax continued with the physical and didn't ask me about my messed-up work life again. He mentioned something about hay fever, recommended a nighttime tea that he enjoyed and wished me a happy birthday. I couldn't believe that another person seemed to know that information, but then I remembered that he had my date of birth in front of him on the screen.

"Are you doing anything to celebrate?" he asked.

"My mom is throwing me a party at Fives. You're welcome to come, I'm not sure what time she said it started." At that, my phone buzzed to say, *Ready when you are!*, from my mom. I guess she anticipated my question or read my mind somehow. I didn't have time to get changed which was a downer.

"Fives?" Dax asked.

"Yeah, the bar. Well, it's called, '*It's five o'clock somewhere*', but no one says the full name," I laughed. I remembered his limited social life and figured he might have never been to the bar.

"Oh yeah, it's across the street, right? I'm either home or here, I don't get out much. Have you been wearing that the entire time?" he asked. I looked down and realized I was now wearing a red dress that miraculously didn't clash with the flame orange of my hair. Dax had been typing on his computer and hadn't been looking at me. How was I wearing this? I was now doubting that I knew what I had been wearing when I arrived.

"Uh… of course," I said. "What else would I have been wearing?"

He chuckled to himself and shook his head. "Sorry. Like I said, I've had a rough few days, ignore me. I am a good doctor, I promise!"

"I believe you," I smiled. We finished up and I walked out of his office and he made an excuse as to why he probably couldn't come to the party. He seemed to still be that shy kid from anatomy class after all these years. The sudden outfit change was baffling, but it didn't change the fact that I had to hurry on over to *Fives* for this party my mom was throwing for me.

The receptionist was on the phone as I was leaving.

"Yes, he's here, he's with a patient right now. Is it urgent?" She paused as she listened to the person on the other end of the line. "Wait? You've found her? He needs to identify the… oh gosh. I can't be the one to tell him!"

I didn't realize it, but I was more of an eavesdrop than I realized. I caught sight of my reflection in the practice windows and saw I was nearly at a forty-five degree angle with my ear towards the desk. The receptionist suddenly pulled the phone away from her ear and covered the mouthpiece. "Did you need something, miss?" she asked.

"No, I was just leaving, sorry!" I said as I rushed out the door.

Stepping onto the sidewalk I wished I could hear the rest of that conversation. It sounded like black belt level gossip, the kind you just couldn't stop yourself from listening in on.

Little did I know I'd hear all about it soon enough.

4

The bar looked crowded from outside, how had my mom gotten this place so packed? I'd imagined a quiet night at her place with some takeout and the cake I had bought from Autumn's. Now that I thought about it, I didn't even know where I had left that thing, had I taken it to the flower shop? Or left it at the bakery? I shouldn't be in charge of anything. This scene right here was like something from one of my daydreams. It was an actual party, with people that liked me. It was just a shame I was dog tired.

I stepped through the door and the people inside all turned to face me before shouting, 'Happy birthday!' in unison. I could hear corks popping around the room and my mom ran at me through a group of people to hug me. We had barely been apart an hour.

"How was Dax?!" she asked.

"Fine. Weird, quiet, just like he was in high school. Pretty uneventful really. When can I get some sleep?" I asked.

"Astrid! Your mother pulled together a party last minute for her only child's birthday!" Cherry barked. "Do the decent thing and have fun will you?!" A few people nearby laughed but I knew she was serious. I hadn't known Cherry before today, but I already understood that she was a force to be reckoned with.

"What would you like to drink?" mom said to me.

"Could I get a coke?" I asked. The room fell silent.

"This is a small town kiddo, we don't drink that city pig swill!" Cherry scorned.

"Soda?" I said, unsure what I had done to draw the ire of an entire room at my own party.

"That's what they want you to think!" mom said. She leaned in and whispered. "The town had a bad experience with a soda business a few years ago. None of us have forgotten. Just go with it."

"Maybe just a water for now then, I haven't drunk much today and I feel a headache coming on." My mom obliged and ordered me a water. I sat at the bar for a while and soaked up the atmosphere of the party, watching while Cherry commandeered the stage and the bar's karaoke machine. It seemed to give her some sort of energy boost, and before long she was on top of a table wailing along to *Islands in the Stream.*

I caught up with a fair share of people but was quite happy just to sit back and watch the entertainment from afar. Then I heard someone say my name.

"Astrid?" I turned to face a slim woman with glossy brown curls that she had half tied up in a bun. The strands that fell free stretched down to her midriff and I recognized her instantly.

"Rachel?!" I squealed. I motioned to throw my arms around her, but she recoiled.

"Dude, I've been exercising. You do *not* want to get sweat on that dress, birthday girl," she smiled. Rachel was my high school best friend. We had kept in touch initially when I moved away but then life got in the way. I hadn't spoken to her for years and we had lived in each other's pockets at one point, seeing her face made me feel glad to be home.

"Urgh, you're a runner now?" I teased.

"Got to do it. My family never did any exercise at all, my mom can barely lift a can of soup from a cupboard now, look at *your* mom," she said. I turned and saw that my mom was now on the table with Cherry, they were jigging wildly, and I hoped that the wood wouldn't collapse beneath them. My mom dyed her hair the color of red wine and it was looking especially rich in the dim light.

"Yeah, physically she's on top form. Mentally...not sure about that," I joked. "So, what have you been doing since we last spoke?"

"Where do I even start? I got a job in the library. It's actually great, it sounds like it might be boring and a few years ago I would have thought the same thing, but I love it," Rachel declared, clearly elated to talk about her job. I hoped I would get that much satisfaction from a job again; I had been feeling hopeless since losing my last one.

"Can I get you a birthday drink?" she asked.

"I'm good for now, but thanks," I said, holding up my water sheepishly.

I watched Rachel stretch across the bar to request a drink. It was busy in the room and quite a few people were waiting to be served. A minute or two passed and everyone around her got an order, but not one single bar tender acknowledged her at all. Was it the sports wear? She had on a t-shirt and runner's tights, not exactly glamorous but it was showing off her figure in a way that I would have thought grabbed other people's attention. After another minute or so I leaned over the bar myself and shouted towards the guy closest to us.

"Hey, numb nuts!" I hollered. He quickly turned around. "What are you having Rach?"

"Limoncello," she said to me while laughing nervously to herself. "I knew I should have showered before coming here!"

I relayed the order to the bartender and he quickly made the drink. I slid it across the counter to Rachel, and we fell back into our conversation.

"Are you dating anyone?" Rachel asked.

"Nope. My love life is just a sad story about making eye contact across a crowded subway car and then never seeing that person again. You?"

"Well I actually—" Rachel began, but was almost immediately distracted by my mother wheeling out a giant cake on a table with wheels.

"Come and blow out your candles, sweetie!" my mother screamed.

It seemed that she was riding the same karaoke energy high as Cherry. The pair of them were like toddlers with a key to a candy factory.

I hopped off the bar stool and walked towards the cake. I could smell orange as I leaned closer and realized that my mom had gotten my favorite flavor.

Despite all the times she cuts me off, it turned out she had been listening all along. I approached the burning candle and she whispered, "Make your wish count!" and I closed my eyes. What could I wish for? I had a mother that clearly loved me and my old best friend from high school was here.

I could wish that Evan fell in love with me or that I won the lottery? That was a little farfetched. I decided to wish for a career that would make me happy, that wasn't unreasonable, right? Rachel clearly had that, Dax was a doctor, Evan was hot...I mean, a police officer. Everyone else had grown up and become something better. Everyone except me.

Once I had blown out the candle, there was a quick applause and then the dancing continued. I looked back over at the bar and Rachel had gone, maybe she was just in the bathroom. I clambered back up onto the bar stool and decided to wait. She didn't return after fifteen minutes. Maybe there was a long line? I went to the bathroom myself and there was nobody there.

She had really struggled to get served at the bar; she probably just went home to change into something that showed off a little skin so that she wouldn't be ignored again. Yeah, that would be it. I hoped that I could find someone else to talk to, but they were all too busy fawning over Cherry and my mom as they danced from table to table.

Some of the faces looked familiar, others were total strangers. People didn't tend to move to Raven Bay, you were just born here and never left. Plenty of small towns are like that, they don't create the mentality that you could just move. I was one of the lucky ones to get out and explore, even though I had obviously come right back like a boomerang.

I was drinking water alone at the bar on my birthday. I kept looking back at the door hoping that Rachel might appear, but she didn't. I noticed that she hadn't even touched the drink I got for her; in fact it was still on the bar in the very same place I had left it.

Weird.

After a while I decided I was feeling pretty tired after a long day and that I wanted to get some sleep. I made my way through the crowded bar to the table where Cherry and my mom were dancing.

"I think I'm gonna have to go home," I yawned.

"But it's your party!" mom squeaked.

"Look at her eyes, Aster. She's barely alive," Cherry laughed. "Give her the key, we can keep going. I've got plenty left in the tank."

My mom reached into her purse and handed me the keys. I looked back up at her with confused eyes as I had no idea where I was going.

"I set up a little apartment for you above the flower shop. I figured you would want a *bit* of personal space and moving back into your childhood bedroom might be a bit much for you, you know, emotionally," she explained.

I was exhausted, I would have slept on the sidewalk if I had to. I nodded gratefully and shouted goodbye to her, then waved to the room as I hurried out of the door and onto the street. I could see the flower shop on the corner, it was so close yet so far away. All I had to do was make it down there, and find my bed before I fell asleep.

I took two steps before I heard a police siren behind me, I turned to see the car rolling to a stop beside the sidewalk. It continued to crawl along until it caught up to me, the window sliding down to reveal Evan's handsome face. He looked good, sure, but this wasn't a good time to tell him what a stone-cold fox he was in that uniform.

"Attie, are you okay? You shouldn't walk about alone, not this late," he said, concern evident in his voice.

"I'm just walking to my mom's flower shop right there," I said. "Raven Bay is the safest place on earth, nothing bad happens here." Evan smiled but the car continued to follow me.

"I'll just escort you down the road like this if you don't mind. I can't drive away until I know you're safe. I fixed your taillight by the way," he mumbled.

"My hero!" I cheered. We were almost there now and despite it being a bit unorthodox, I appreciated that he was worried about me. I unlocked the front door of the flower shop and turned to Evan in the car behind me. "Do you want a little orchid for your dash? It would really brighten up the inside of your vehicle," I chuckled. He smiled back at me. Was this flirting?

"Lock the door once you get in, promise me," he said.

"Yes, Sir," I replied with a mock salute. "Nighty night, Officer Brooks." I locked the door behind me and looked out across the shop floor. I didn't actually know how to get to the apartment above the store, and my mom hadn't given me any helpful instructions, but the small door behind the kiosk felt like the right way to me.

I ducked around the counter and went through the door, on the other side there was a staircase leading up and one leading down. I remembered mom said something about a witches meeting in the basement and I laughed to myself; she sure was crazy. I climbed up the stairs, and found another door, which opened with the same key. The door opened into a pretty large apartment.

Was this all for me? *Jeez*, I had really lucked out!

The main lights came on automatically and illuminated the living room that I was in, blinding me momentarily. I continued to drag my feet across the floor like a zombie and fell face first onto a large plush sofa.

Looking over I saw a glass of water, that I could have sworn was not there a moment ago, now sat on the coffee table in front of me.

I reached forward and gladly poured it into my mouth, gulping it down until the glass was empty. The TV burst to life and I wondered if I had leant against the remote control, I looked around but saw that it was resting on the TV stand. Weird.

The local news title sequence had just ended and a very serious looking woman behind a desk began to speak.

'Good evening! Tonight, we begin with news that the identity of the mystery body by the lake has been released. Two days ago, a female jogger was discovered at the edge of Raven Bay, she has today been formally identi-fied by a family member and we can confirm that it is the body of local librarian Rachel Bailey."

I suddenly sat up straight and blinked at the TV, pinching myself as I wondered if this was a dream or not. The image of my curly haired best friend then appeared on the screen beside the reporter. The very same friend that I had just seen at Fives only an hour ago.

As the news continued, I blocked it out, trying to figure out just what the heck was going on.

None of this made any sense. I had just been speaking with Rachel at the bar.

How could she have been dead for two days?!

5

I felt the heaviness of sleep lift from me and realized I was still on the sofa. I must have fallen asleep here after the news last night. I hadn't even explored the apartment properly like I had wanted to. All I could think about was my friend, dead by the lake, but somehow also at my birthday party.

A hard decision faced me: either surrender to the idea that I have had a psychotic break after the stress of the last week, or begin to believe that I was a witch, one that could apparently see ghosts. I was a rational person; it was time to convince myself one way or the other.

I rearranged myself on the sofa so that I was sat up straight and noticed that I was in my pajamas. I hadn't been wearing them out to the bar, so somehow, I had changed my clothes. I thought of the incident at the doctor's office with my party dress, these would go under the 'Maybe I *am* a witch' column on my mental tally chart.

The news said that Rachel was dead, but I *had* seen her. She had rejected my hug on the basis that she would be too sweaty, that was normal though right? The cheerleader in the flower shop had reached out to stop me falling and my hand had gone right through her arm, would this have happened if I had tried to hug Rachel?

She was a gorgeous woman, absolutely stunning, and not one

single bartender was giving her the slightest bit of attention to get her a drink. Was this because no one else could see her? Darn it, there were quite a few points for the argument that I was a ghost-seeing witch.

I needed to go and see Rachel's family for myself, or at least observe from a respectful distance to see what was going on. Maybe I could visit the library. If Rachel was alive then she was probably at work. I would put an end to this mystery one way or the other.

I stood up and walked towards the kitchen. The apartment was open so that the only separate rooms were the bedrooms and bathroom. It was cute in here; I could see my mom's influence on the decorating in an instant. She hated colorful walls. I think it had been some interior design show in the 90's that had been big into a 'feature wall' that sent her over the edge. She wanted white paint on every surface.

She had framed pictures of random shapes—I suspected they were the stock images that came with the frames—and she had hung them on the wall above the sofa. I would have to add a more personal touch if this was going to be my place long term.

The knee-jerk reaction to having to move back here was that it would be temporary and that I would work my butt off to get back on my feet and away from here. I didn't feel that urgency anymore, even though it had only been a day. I felt comfortable here, despite the potential ghost-seeing ability I had discovered.

The kitchen was small. It was shaped like a horseshoe with one side open so that you could look out to the dining area. The whole place was so much nicer than the apartment I had in the city. Everything was more spaced out, it felt like you could relax here. I wondered if my mom had decorated all this in the few days since we arranged for me to come back to Raven Bay.

I had figured I would be moving back into my old room at her house, she would have had to move at a thousand miles an hour to get this place looking so good so fast. *Unless she really is a witch.* I needed to eat. I pulled open the fridge and it was fully stocked. My stomach was growling, all I could remember eating yesterday was cake.

I had cake at a gas station diner, an orange roll at Autumn's bakery, I grabbed another cake to go but lost it, and then eaten cake at the bar. My body needed something savory before my blood sugar levels put me into a coma.

Sitting in the fridge, among the eggs, butter, vegetables and sodas, was my boxed-up cake from Autumn. How had it made it up here? I grabbed the eggs and some cheese, placed them on the counter and leaned back in to see what else I could put into an omelet. I picked up the butter and decided I would just have a few slices of toast with it instead of making things complicated.

It was a salve for my mind to focus on the preparation of my breakfast for ten minutes rather than the chaos of the world around me. I listened to the omelet mixture sizzle in the pan, the smell of the cheese melting as I sprinkled the grated pieces over the egg. Spreading the butter across warm, fresh bread that had just bounced out of the toaster. It was like a mini vacation.

I carried my food to the round dining table that was only a few steps away from the stove, walked back to pour myself a glass of orange juice before finally sitting down to my meal. The window beside the table had the blinds open and the sunlight was filtering in enough to add a golden hue to the room. I hoped to not see anything crazy on the street down below, I scooted the chair at an angle so I couldn't catch sight of a ghost or a werewolf on the sidewalk.

I took the first bite of toast and closed my eyes to savor the silence; it was short lived.

"I thought you might at least cry a little!" I almost choked on my food as I flinched in response to the sudden talking of a familiar voice. Rachel was sitting across the table from me, still in her workout gear.

"What?" I said, regaining control of myself.

"You were told last night by the news lady that I was dead, done, over, finished, and here you are eating eggs. Girl, you're unbelievable!" she smiled.

"H-How did you get in here?" I stammered.

"Attie, I died. It's real. Stressful right? Try being me!" she was sitting with her arms folded and grinning at me. This had to be a joke.

She acknowledged the look on my face and eased her body language. "I'm sorry I bailed on your party last night, I've only been dead a few days and I haven't really got the hang of the whole 'spiritual form' thing yet. It's hard not having magic now I'm dead."

"Wait. You're a witch too?" I asked.

"I *was* a witch, yeah. I know you missed out on a lot of it because you moved away. Now that you're back though, all your powers should kick in and you will see just how much fun it is. You've just got to stay alive!" she laughed.

"They said your name was Rachel Bailey, did you get married?" Her last name had been 'Howe' when we were in school together. I only knew one 'Bailey' family around here.

"Yeah, Dax is my husband! Dax Bailey? He's a doctor now!" she grinned. She lifted up her left hand, presumably to admire the rings that lived there, but she wasn't wearing any jewelry. "What the heck? Where are my diamonds?"

"You married Dax? Nerdy Dax? Wow, maybe *I* am the one that died," I chuckled. We had thought he was such a dweeb, or at least I had.

"Attie, don't joke. I am legitimately dead! But yes, I married Dax and I haven't had the guts to float myself back to the house to check on him. I can't imagine the pain he is going through, he must be in pieces," she lamented.

She didn't know that I had seen Dax yesterday and that he had been at work, acting as if nothing was going on. He had mentioned that he was having a rough few days, but otherwise he seemed fine. Why would a man who had a missing wife be going about his life as if nothing was wrong?

"How did you die?" I said. The words fired out of my mouth before I had the chance to consider their appropriateness.

"You don't waste time, do you?" she laughed again. "I don't know, to cut a long story short. I guess I had felt unwell for a few days, nothing too strange about that. I decided a run would clear my head and I remember lacing up my sneakers and getting out of the house, then my memory cuts off. The last week or so has felt patchy actually."

"Do you have any ideas? Like, did you have a heart problem or something?" I probed. I couldn't think of another reason why a young woman would collapse and die while out jogging.

"Nope," she said. "We may never know." Rachel paused and looked out the window. "This is probably going to sound weird, but... I think someone might have killed me."

"By the lake?" I asked, setting my fork down as I leaned in closer to the conversation.

She shook her head. "No. I don't think so. I mean, it's hazy. But... I don't know. I have this feeling. It's hard to explain. It's like there's a question that needs answering, and something keeps pushing me towards you."

"Me?"

"Yeah."

"What have I got to do with any of this?" I asked.

"You're an investigative journalist, right? I bet this sort of thing is right up your alley!"

"I *was* an investigative journalist, but I only really covered the stories. I wasn't the one out there solving the crimes. That's what the police do."

"Attie, I have a *feeling* here. Okay. I think someone maybe did hurt me, and maybe you're the one that's going to help figure things out!" I sat back in my chair again, unsure if I felt the same way. "If you don't do it for me, then do it for Dax. He'll be distraught about this, he's such a sensitive soul."

I wasn't sure I had the heart to tell Rachel that Dax didn't seem bothered in the slightest. That made me sit up straight.

"What is it?" Rachel asked.

"Huh? Nothing. Well..."

"Well?"

I left the rest of the thought unfinished, but my mind was already running away from me. Dax *had* been unusually calm yesterday, and I'd seen a few cases where a husband acting calm in the face of tragedy was never a good sign.

It led to the question of motive though. Dax was mild-mannered and polite, but there could be a thousand things that triggered someone into murdering their betrothed. Money. Love. Marriage. Divorce. Maybe Rachel had a huge life insurance policy.

"Well, I think we're rushing into things here," I said. "People drop dead sometimes. Not everything in life is a giant mystery."

She narrowed her eyes at me, smiling all the while. "You haven't changed a bit. I can tell you think something is up. What is it?"

"What is it?!" another voice said from across the room. I looked over and saw a small black cat sitting neatly by the door that lead to the staircase. "I'll tell you what's up! You guys made breakfast and didn't invite me!"

What the—

"It talked!" I said, my mouth agape as I watched the feline prowl across the apartment to the kitchen table.

"Who's it? The cat's mother?!" the cat said, laughing as it sat on the floor by the table. "Nice to finally meet you Attie, I'm Siren, but just call me Renny. Everyone else does."

6

___

a talking cat? Chalk that one under the 'psychotic break' column on my tally list. I was just sitting here enjoying my breakfast, chatting to a ghost about her potential murder, and was interrupted by a talking cat. I didn't need this on top of everything else.

"Can you hear that cat?" I asked Rachel.

"Ren? Oh yeah, he is probably wondering why you only made breakfast for one!" she smiled.

"I am indeed, not off to a great start, are we?!" he meowed. His jet-black fur was glossy, and he didn't have a single fleck of white anywhere. He approached the table and rubbed up against my leg. I heard the thunder of footsteps running up the stairs and Cherry burst through the door.

"Renny, I said to stay downstairs! Let the girl eat in peace for crying out loud!" Cherry barked. I realized in her eyes I was sitting alone. Little did she know I was entertaining the ghost of my recently departed friend and this breakfast was anything but relaxing.

"Aren't you going to introduce me?" Renny asked, looking in Cherry's direction.

"Urgh, fine. This is Siren, he is a cat. He is the coven cat; he lives in this building and now that you live here too, I guess you are room-mates. He is a bossy little thing and you can just pretend you can't hear him if he is bothering you," Cherry said, taking a bow once she finished.

"I did not care for that," Renny groaned. "But it is mostly correct. And you are?" He was looking up at Rachel.

"Rachel Bailey, I died this week," she answered nonchalantly.

"My condolences," he said, bowing his head.

"You can see her?" I asked him.

"Yeah, up until you showed up, Renny was the only way for us to know what was going on in the ghost community. That's how we knew about the cheerleader girl," Cherry said. "Weren't you and Rachel close a while back?"

"Yeah. Something is off about the whole thing, I don't feel right about her just dropping dead by the lake, that seems weird to me," I murmured, mostly to myself.

"Follow your gut sweetheart, these things won't unravel them-selves. Come on Renny, leave them be." Cherry held the door open and Renny reluctantly joined her as she descended back down to the flower shop below.

"What do you think Rach? I'm going to need to snoop around a bit to see if this is something we need to be worried about," I said.

"Do what you got to do," she smiled. "I wish I could remember more; my memory feels a little hazy. When is my funeral? Is it weird if I come with you? I could be your plus one!"

"Ha. I don't actually know when it is, I have only known you were dead for just under twelve hours, I'll ask around." I picked up my toast and even though it was now cold, it still helped to fill up the empty space in my stomach that I had been neglecting. I wanted to shower before I went out on a crime solving mission too.

"I'll just wander about, I'll find you later," Rachel said before dissolving into the air and disappearing entirely. She must have antic-ipated that I would need to go and do some other things. I didn't get up straight away. I needed a moment to process everything that had happened in the last half hour.

It was much harder to ignore the fact that I might be a witch, a real witch. There was a talking cat in the mix now, ghosts left, right and center and I would just have to accept it quickly and get into the business of investigating Rachel's death.

I sighed then took myself off towards the bedroom to investigate the space. I spotted my suitcase and as I pulled open the closet doors, saw that all of my clothes had been neatly put away. The bathroom was a similar story, my toothbrush was sitting in a pot beside the sink and my shower products were lined up beside a fluffy white towel.

I had lost the will to act surprised, so showered while contemplating my first move with regards to the investigation. I wondered if Dax would have shown up to work today, maybe I should start there. I rinsed off the suds and shut off the water, grabbing the towel and wrapping it around my body.

Renny was waiting in the bedroom when I walked in to grab some clean clothes. I flinched when he moved out of the corner of my eye.

"You again," I smiled. "How is your morning going so far?" I didn't know how to initiate a conversation with a cat so I would have to figure that out as I went along.

"It's been fine. That dead cheerleader is moping about downstairs again, she wants carnations now. She is exhausting," he moaned. "So, you think Rachel was murdered?"

"Maybe. Do you?" I replied.

"Yes. She was a witch; witches don't randomly die of natural causes at this age. What are we going to do about it?" He stretched his paws out long in front of himself, sticking his butt up in the air and flicking his tail.

"We? *I* am planning to look into her husband and ask around at the library where she worked. Any other suggestions?" I had a smaller towel in my hands and used it to rub at my hair to soak up the moisture, my hair looked a dark red when it was wet, almost the same color as my mom's. When it dried it would be the vibrant orange I was used to.

"Maybe ask your police friend?" he mumbled. "I want to be involved too, you're not the only one who can see ghosts."

"Won't it be weird if I take a cat to the library?" I asked.

"I go there all the time, people around here don't even notice." I continued getting dressed as Renny told me stories about himself and the women in the coven that he was a part of, nothing informative really, just which ones gave him the tastiest snacks when the others weren't looking. It sounded like the coven was bigger than I had first thought.

I pulled on a pair of jeans and grabbed a white t-shirt. I felt compelled to avoid patterns on account of my hair, I could never find anything that didn't violently clash with my coloring. It felt warm out so I closed the closet doors without grabbing a jacket and threw my hair up into a ponytail so that it wouldn't get stuck underneath the shoulder straps of my backpack.

"How does this work then? Do I carry you? Are there going to be non-witch people there that think it's weird to have a cat in a library?" I asked.

"I can walk, thank you very much," he chirruped. "I have been marching around these streets longer than you, missy. People love me here, no one bats an eye anymore when I enter a building. It's so regular it is borderline tedious."

We walked down the stairs to find Evan waiting in the flower shop below. I felt nervous all of a sudden, but I hadn't done anything wrong. Why was he here though?

"Good morning," I said. "What brings you here at this hour, Sir?" I felt like I had forgotten how normal people from this century spoke to each other. I couldn't remember what a casual stance looked like, I stood with my feet wider than my shoulders and my arms folded as if he was about to get rejected from entering a nightclub.

"I have your keys. I fixed the taillight, like I said last night. Although you emptied out all your stuff, so you obviously have a spare," he smiled, handing me the key.

"Yeah, *obviously*," I smiled back. I suspected magic had been involved but I couldn't say it out loud. "Thank you for this, I really appreciate it."

"I'm happy to help," he replied. No one spoke for several seconds and I could hear my pulse drumming in my ears, yearning to hear his voice again.

"What happened to Rachel?" I said, so desperate for the conversation to continue with the handsome man that I said something I should have kept to myself. He took half a step closer to me and I felt tingly all over.

"I can't really talk about that, but there's some odd stuff going on around here and it's keeping us busy," he said. I looked into his eyes, searching for more information, but none came.

"Like what?" I asked.

"You didn't hear this from me," he whispered. "But earlier this week a woman and her daughter were rushed to the hospital with stomach cramps that were driving them both to tears, they were vomiting a lot too. Dax is their primary physician, he reported that he thought there was food poisoning going around or something."

I knew how this went. In a situation like this, those two people would be asked to write down everything they remember eating or drinking recently and then the process of elimination would lead them to one store, or one restaurant, or even their own kitchen. These procedures had the potential to get ahead of a local health crisis.

"Do you think that Rachel died from food poisoning?" I asked, unsure.

"No idea, hard to know if she had any of the same symptoms at this point. It's being looked into, that's as much as I can say," Evan said. He was looking deep into my blue eyes and I wondered if I had used some sort of magical ability to get him to say all that to me. This was an open investigation and he had given me a couple of giant leads.

"Attie, when do you want the full tour?" my mom announced loudly from the other side of the room. I looked over and she had just come in from the rear door, she didn't seem concerned that I was mid-conversation with a police officer.

"I was just about to—" I began.

"Now works for me too, let's go!" she shouted, using a large sweeping motion of her arm to get me to join her.

"I'll see you later, hopefully," Evan said. I didn't respond. I watched him walk out of the front of the store and get into his patrol car. When he was driving away, I whispered, *see you soon,* to myself.

"That was embarrassing," Renny cackled. "It's like you haven't spoken to a guy before."

"Leave me alone!" I said, blushing.

"That's her high school crush, Renny. These things don't ever die," mom smiled. My cheeks flushed hot with the cringeworthy situation I was a part of, I needed something to take everybody's mind off my love life, or lack of it. I walked across the shop floor and joined my mom by the door. "Should we start with the worktable?"

"Sure," I agreed. We walked around the edge of a flower display to a desk that was clearly used to prepare the bouquets; equipped with ribbon, plastic, note cards and scissors.

"A lot of the time, people don't know what they want," mom explained. "They come in and point at a few things and expect you to work some sort of magic. Fortunately, here we can do exactly that. If you step here to the...Cherry!"

My mom crouched down beside Cherry who was lying unconscious behind the worktable. She was breathing, I could see that from here, but she wouldn't open her eyes. I pulled out my cell phone to call for an ambulance. Maybe Evan was right, something *was* going on around here and it was bad news for all of us.

herry was waking up, but not fully. She was groaning in pain and clutching at her abdomen. My mom was cradling her and whispering something. Was she using magic? I had no idea what that even looked like. I knew that she would be desperate to save her friend. I had only just gotten here, and I was so attached to Cherry already.

"The dispatcher said they are almost here," I said, clutching my phone tightly to my ear to make sure I didn't miss any instructions. The front doors flew open as two EMTs rushed into the room and saw me waving dramatically to show them our location. It felt like a blur of uniforms and equipment rushed by me and my mom stepped back to give them space.

"I'll be going to the hospital with her, Attie. I need you to take care of things here," she said. I nodded with a keenness to be helpful but didn't have the first clue about plants and was hoping that nobody came into the store when I was alone. "Don't eat or drink anything," she instructed. "I think someone is trying to rip apart the coven!"

After that bombshell statement, she followed the medical crew out to the ambulance with Cherry and I stood silently watching them through the glass doors. They would be hooking Cherry up to machines or taking measurements or something, then they would drive away. What was going on around here? Rachel had been killed, a mother and daughter were possibly poisoned, and now Cherry? My mom might be on to something.

The vehicle rumbled in place, then drove away up the street towards the hospital. I was now the only one here and the quiet was frightening.

"You'll be fine," Renny purred at my ankle. "We can visit the library later."

"That's not what I'm worried about. I had thought that it was just a *'the husband did it'* thing, but now I'm not so sure," I replied.

"Well get it together quickly, the gang is here," he said, before bounding across the floor and jumping up onto the counter beside the cash register. The bell above the door rang as a large group of women entered all at once.

"Attie," one of them shouted as she turned the 'open' sign around to read 'closed', before locking the door. "Let's go."

"We are open, I can't...where are you going?" I tried to ascertain who these people were, but they were marching past Renny and straight towards the stairs. They were heading down to the basement. After the last one of them disappeared out of sight, Renny jumped down to follow them. I jogged to catch up. By the time I was at the bottom of the stairs they were sitting in a circle on chairs and chatting loudly.

"Attie, would you like to go first?" someone shouted.

"Sorry, I don't mean to be rude here, but I don't know what is going on. I am supposed to be running the place because—"

"Because your mom took Cherry to the hospital," someone interrupted. How could they know that already? It happened less than ten minutes ago. The interrupter stood up to address me. "I'm Lilly, would you like me to head the meeting for today?" I nodded softly and sat on an empty chair.

"Okay everyone, this is what we have so far," Lilly began. She stepped over to a whiteboard that I hadn't previously noticed that was hanging on the wall, pulled out a pen from her pocket and then released her grip. The pen hovered several feet above the ground and I kept blinking to try and understand what I was seeing. As she spoke the pen began to make notes.

"Rachel Bailey is dead. Elizabeth and Lola Smith were hospitalized earlier this week, and now Cherry. They are all members of this coven, any guesses as to what's going on?" Lilly asked. The pen was drawing pictures of each woman she had just referred to, Cherry's picture made me laugh out loud for some reason, it was probably because of the flamboyant pair of glasses the pen had added to her face.

"Did they all get stabbed?" an older lady yelled.

"No, Gail, not everything is a stabbing!" Lilly reprimanded. A few of the other women tutted in Gail's direction.

"Poisoning," I said. "Officer Brooks told me that they think the mom and daughter had some sort of poisoning."

"Attie, yes! A million high-fives for you," Lilly said, nodding towards the pen that wrote 'poison' underneath Elizabeth and Lola's images. "Rachel too?"

"They don't know yet, I think they are looking into it. But it might be what got Cherry, right?" I suggested.

"Hmm, quite possible. That's enough brain power for now, let's brunch!" Lilly gestured over my shoulder and I turned to see that a long table running along one wall was now covered in fresh food; fruit, pastries, bacon, eggs and a five-bean chili that had been labeled with 'spice level: extreme'. The women stood and began marching towards the table like zombies.

"No wait!" I shouted, jumping up and using my body as a physical barrier between them and the food. "My mom said I shouldn't eat or drink anything until she gets back. She thinks someone is poisoning the coven!" I felt silly using the word 'coven', but it was what everyone else was saying and I was trying to join in.

"Oh crumbs," Lilly groaned. She clicked her fingers and the table burst into flames. I screamed, but before I could look around for a fire extinguisher, the flames died out and the table was gone. My heart was beating so fast, I had already pictured having to tell my mom that

I had burned down her business almost as soon as she left. I needed a moment to recover.

"People think witches hate fire because of the whole 'burnt at the stake' business," Gail whispered to me. "But we love setting fire to stuff just as much as everybody else." Well that was alarming.

"What's next then?" Lilly said. "Attie, I'm talking to you."

"Oh, I guess I need to see if I can find out what these women all consumed before they got sick. I don't know how to get hold of Rachel, she just shows up," I chuckled. No one else laughed.

"You have 'the sight'?" somebody asked.

"We heard a rumor but, wow," Lilly said, smiling at me with pride as if I had done something impressive. "Well we will put you in charge of it then, the police don't work quickly enough, and you have access to an extra witness! Also, Liz and Lola will speak to you, they *hate* the cops."

Everyone nodded in agreement at this presumably common knowledge about their police-hating coven sisters. How could I oversee an investigation? I wasn't technically qualified to do anything like that, I had experience with it, but never in any real official capacity.

"Any other business then?" Gail asked.

"Let me see, we covered dead witch, three sick witches...we skipped brunch, that normally takes up about forty minutes," Lilly mumbled to herself. "Oh, well we haven't welcomed Attie to the group!"

The room erupted into whooping and cheering, I nervously waved in response. "Thanks," I stuttered anxiously. This was an intense amount of spotlight on me and I wanted to shrink back into the shadows.

"Have you picked up some books yet?" Gail asked. "We know you left town before your powers kicked in so you will have some major catching up to do."

"Books?" I shrugged.

"Oh honey, your mother probably would have sorted it out for you today, but obviously she is otherwise occupied. Go to the library and if you ask anyone behind the desk for 'the cloves collection', then they will guide you to our special section," she smiled. I liked Gail, she was giving off strong, affectionate grandmother energy and I was enjoying it.

"Okay." I stood taller, trying to carry the weight of all this new information had been causing me to feel physically burdened and I had been hunching over, my back was aching. "So, the library will have books for me?"

"Yes," Gail smiled. "Don't read them all as quickly as possible because you'll exhaust yourself." She winked at me and I thought about whether the winking was a special witch language that I didn't yet understand.

"It's good that you are friendly with a police officer already," Lilly smirked. "It might help you extract more information from him if needs be."

I opened my mouth in preparation of a quickfire defense of myself and how I didn't plan to flirt my way to the solution to the mystery but thought better of it. If the group of witches around me thought that spending more time with Evan would be beneficial, then who am I to try and fight magic wisdom?

Purses were collected from the ground, coats slipped back onto bodies and the witches began to filter out of the basement and back up the stairs. I guess that meant the meeting was over.

"You will do well here, I'm sure," Gail reassured me, resting her hand on the side of my arm. "Your mother is treasured in our community; Cherry will steer you straight and the rest of us will support you. I knew your grandmother, a vicious little battle-axe but a good friend. Have you ever seen an alligator-snapping turtle? They remind me of her."

Gail was smiling now at a memory, I backed away and turned to walk up the stairs. I couldn't remember my grandmother well, either of my grandparents actually. We also never speak about my father, it's this huge elephant in the room and everyone in my family has always been happy to pretend that it isn't something I might like to know more about. Maybe I would learn more about him now that all these secrets were being shared, like how my whole family has magical powers.

When I got back up to the flower shop, some of the witches were browsing the herbs section as others walked out of the front door. There felt like a greater sense of urgency for me now after what had happened to Cherry. If someone had poisoned her, then my investigation could help them figure out what she had been given and then they would know what medicine she needed. I could save her life.

"I'm closing up for the rest of the morning," I announced. There was a low groan from one old woman as she shuffled past me, but the others obliged. Once Lilly and Gail had vacated the basement it was time for me to get to the library. The shop sign still read 'closed', but I didn't know where the key had gone that my mom gave me last night.

"You want to lock up, dear?" Gail asked. She hadn't walked too far away from the door yet and could clearly see me standing there confused.

"She is *very* new to this," Renny meowed from the ground by my feet. I was getting teased by a talking cat, *great*.

"Press your hand to the door and focus on what you want to happen. Like you are taking a huge breath in before blowing out a large candle," Gail instructed. I pressed my palm to the wood beside the lock and did what she asked. I heard the metal shift inside the door. When I tried the handle, it wouldn't budge.

"Good job, missy. You'll be unstoppable in no time!" Gail cheered. I was smiling from ear to ear. It was real. I really had powers and I had just used them, on purpose, to make something happen. Now all I had to do was solve a murder.

I needed to get to the library.

8

$\mathcal{I}$ walked up the street towards the library. There was a gentle incline that didn't seem to bother anybody else, but I was so used to flat city sidewalks that it felt like I was hiking up a mountain. I could still see members of the coven on their way to wherever they were going after the meeting. They were dipping into other businesses and not coming out. It seemed that there might be a witch working in every building.

I walked past the bar, Fives, and wondered if it had been something from the party that had poisoned Cherry. Maybe there would be other cases today that would help us identify the source. Across the street I saw 'Healthcare on The Bay' and some activity inside. Was Dax really working the day after it was confirmed that his wife was dead?

I saw a figure walk by the window and quickly recognized it as the body of the receptionist. I made a mental note to check in on the doctor after my library visit. If he was working today, then he would be my number one suspect. I would have to figure out if he knew the other three poison victims. The library was in sight and I almost tripped over Renny as I sped up.

"You know, it is open for at least another seven hours, there's no rush," he complained.

"Cherry might not have seven more hours," I snapped. "Sorry, I just have a lot on my plate. I have been put in charge of this thing by a group of witches, what happens if I mess up? Do they turn me into a toad? Do they dunk me in the lake to see if I float or not?"

"Where are you getting these ideas from?" he laughed. "They are on your side, as am I, but if you stumble over my fragile little body again then I might change my mind!"

The library was the closest building to the mountains that surrounded the town on two sides, the lake was another border and the road out of town sloped off to flatter land. It was a three-story brick building with arched windows and boxes of flowers under each pane of glass. Pillars rose up out of the ground all the way up to the roof and created a small sheltered area around the outer walls.

It was grand, yet quaint. There were small details that showed that it was looked after, the amount of greenery on the outside was one, the hand stitched fabric banner announcing an author event was another. I walked in with an excitement to see how much it had changed since my last visit.

There must have been at least two dozen people in the library, roaming the shelves or sat at desks frantically taking notes. When I was a high school student I had come here too, I wondered if any of these kids were witches, maybe they were learning magic just like I needed to. Although people were telling me that I had moved away before I came into my powers, it must be an age thing.

"Hi there," a friendly voice said. I looked over at the blonde man that had spoken, I felt tense that he would spot Renny at my heel and ask us to leave. He smiled down at the black cat weaving around me and then started to stare at my face, squinting softly as he did so. "Astrid?"

"Yes?"

"It's Owen! We were in drama club together!" he grinned. "Come on, don't tell me I've been forgotten already?" I stared back at him and then the memories started to pour back into my mind. We had been in a romantic scene together in no less than three productions. We had kissed as part of the play, and I had gotten caught up in the idea that maybe he really liked me, but he started dating Stephanie Bartly and I was heartbroken.

I hoped that my infatuation had been a secret. Looking at him now I could see what I saw then, the sharp jaw, the soft green eyes, but I was still swimming in my reignited crush on Evan. Turns out I liked most of the guys at school, who knew?

"I remember!" I said. "How are you?"

His smile dropped and he pressed his lips together. Dang, I'd forgotten that Rachel worked here. He would be grieving for her too. How did I manage to turn regular interactions into uncomfortable ones so fast? Was that my true magical power?

"I suppose you heard about...?" he began.

"Yeah," I finished, not wanting to hear her name out loud. I still needed time to figure out how to handle her death, even though I was investigating it. "I... I wanted to ask about The Clove..."

"Not him," Renny coughed, stretching up my body and sticking his claws into my leg.

"Hello there, I believe I know what you're looking for. Right this way." A woman that I assumed was in charge came to escort me away from Owen and through a gap between two rows of bookshelves. "I'm Erin, you must be Attie," she said.

"Yes, nice to meet you," I replied. I was watching the back of her head as she navigated me one way, then another, weaving through the shelves until we reached a door. She unlocked the door in the same way that I had locked the flower shop, her hand pressed against the wood. It swung open into a small, windowless room that had a table covered in stacks of books and one chair in the center under a bare bulb.

This looked like an interrogation room from the 1970's. I felt like I was about to be coerced into a confession and I didn't have a lawyer with me. Erin walked into the room and we followed; Renny nudged the door shut once we were inside.

When Erin turned around, I could see her large, square glasses with an orange tint to the lens. I thought of the giant glasses that Cherry wore and thought that perhaps the local optician was placing a mean trick on all of them. Her sandy blonde hair was thick and wild, tucked behind her ears on both sides and only just reaching her jawline.

She was wearing a salmon colored jumper with a patterned scarf. Her whole aesthetic was screaming 'librarian' to me.

"Aster, your mother, did call ahead and explain the situation," Erin explained. "So, I have put out a few introductory texts. I would recommend you take two at the most, these things are not easy it's important not to rush."

"Where do I start?" I asked, looking at the books on the table.

"Honestly?" she laughed. "I'd grab one at random and get out of here. It's a weird, dusty little space and I have completely lost the vacuum cleaner. It gets worse by the day!"

I reached out and snatched the book from the top of the closest pile, 'The Green Guide'. The blurb stated that it was ideal for members of a coven that like to meet outdoors, a delightful handbook for natural magic and the use of herbs, flowers, essential oils and more. With any luck this might help me with the flower shop.

"Great, so just sign inside the front cover and that transposes over to my records," Erin said, handing me a pen. I opened the book and saw that it had a traditional sign out sheet. I had to write today's date and under the column, 'this book was enjoyed by' I had to write my name.

The sign out sheet was a sticker that was added into the book. It had been borrowed so many times that the sticker after sticker had been layered on top of each other until it was almost half an inch thick. I swung my backpack off my shoulders and slipped the book inside.

"Is there anything else you want while you are here? Maybe a general interest book? You look like the type of witch that would enjoy a space adventure novel," she smiled. I *did* like those types of books, but I had something else in mind.

"Do you have any books on poisoning? One that would be available to everyone?" I asked.

Erin thought for a minute, took her glasses off her face and exhaled hot breath onto the lenses before wiping them clean with her scarf. She slid them back into position and then said, "I was just thinking of what we have in stock at the moment. I'll take you to a good section."

We walked back out of the room and Renny hurried after us. The path back out involved the same weaving around bookshelves but soon we were in the main body of the ground floor of the library. I saw Owen look over at us with slight confusion, but a customer needed his attention at the desk, so he turned away to deal with that. Erin guided me up the stairs to the next floor.

"What type of poison are you interested in?" she asked.

"I don't know what the types are," I confessed. I should probably have done even the smallest bit of research before I came here.

"Is this about Cherry?" she whispered, leaning close so that no one else could hear. I nodded. "Well, I will do what I can to help. How about this one?" She plucked a thin book off the shelf titled, 'The Art of Poison; A Murderer's Manual'.

"Thanks," I said, taking it from her. It was probably a long shot, but if we could narrow down what the four victims had in common then we could possibly identify where they were poisoned and what was used. Part of me still wanted this to be a harmless case of food poisoning, but Rachel had died from it. Had anyone ever died from food poisoning before? I should probably look that up too.

"That one you will need to scan out at the desk downstairs," Erin informed me. "Owen can sort that out for you no problem. I do hope that you are able to get to the bottom of this." She turned to assist some teenagers that were struggling with their French homework and I made my way back down the stairs.

When I was researching pieces for the paper it would often involve teaching myself something completely new. I had needed to write an article on the consequences of identity theft, I had started with books that touched on the topic, then narrowed down my searches to include financial crimes and then ended with the introduction of certain clauses in insurance policies.

I hoped that starting with a random book on poisons might help guide my research to figure out what had happened to Cherry. I needed to know if the rest of us were in danger too. Would someone try to poison me? Or my mom? I made it down to the ground floor again and when I got to the desk, slid the book across to Owen.

He scanned the barcode on the back and asked me to fill out a quick form to re-instate my old library card. It had expired since my last borrowing.

"Ooh, you got lucky with this one," Owen smiled.

"Did I?" I said, my eyebrow raised.

"Oh yeah, Dr Bailey just returned it yesterday." Owen carried on typing into his computer and I tried to stop my jaw from hitting the floor. Dr Bailey? Rachel's husband had *just* been reading about poison the week that she died, that was a red flag. I opened the front cover, there was a little sign out sticker in this one too for some reason.

I looked at all the names that had signed out the book, I realized that he wasn't the only one that had been reading it. Why were so many people in this town interested in murder by poison?

9

I read the name over and over, hoping to have mistaken the individual letters. No. It still read, *'Dr. Bailey'*, no matter how many times I looked at it. Owen was patiently waiting for me to snap out of whatever daze I was lost in and finally coughed gently to get my attention.

"Sorry," I said, looking back up from the book. "Thank you." I put my backpack onto the counter and stowed the book away next to the witch text, replaced the bag on my back and walked out of the library. Renny followed along but I glanced down and could see him staring up at me curiously, he didn't know the significance of what we had found.

"You have the expression of someone who experienced an 'ah-hah!' moment," he said once we were outside.

"Rachel was potentially killed because of an exposure to poison, we *know* that the two women hospitalized were poisoned and now something has happened to Cherry that looks similar. I suspect that the people we need to investigate are the very same people that are listed in the front of that book, Dr. Bailey is one of them."

"Who else is there?" he asked.

"I recognized Autumn and Gail, that worries me. Both of them seem so friendly and I have no reason to think they are dangerous, but..." I began, trailing off as I walked down the street. I saw Dax walking into his office from the sidewalk, Autumn's daughter walking towards the bakery and Gail wandering into a shoe store.

"Trust no one, that's the cat way," he purred. My backpack starting buzzing and I crouched down to stand it on the ground as I dug inside for my cellphone. It was my mom.

"Hey!" I answered.

"Hello sweetheart how is the store?" she asked. I thought she might ask how *I* was first, but now we know the order of priority. I could see the store from where I was, and it didn't look like it had been obliterated from this distance.

"Fine, all good here. How is Cherry?"

"Well it looks like she has some sort of food poisoning or something. The doctor said the symptoms match up with a few other cases they have seen in the last week," she explained.

"How many cases exactly?" This was getting out of control.

"I think he said Cherry brings it up to six." So, *if* Rachel had been poisoned too, then that was seven. I had to work out what they all had in common if I was going to get to the bottom of this. I wondered if they were all the targets of this mystery poisoner. Who could have a vendetta against that many people at once?

"What were the symptoms?" I asked.

"Cherry has obviously got stomach cramps, she was sweating, honestly I think she is hallucinating, and she definitely seems confused," mom said. I thought of Rachel saying that she had felt confused in the days leading up to her death. I needed to speak to her again.

"Thanks mom, I'm going to look into this more, something bigger is going on and it needs to be stopped. Tell Cherry I am sending her good thoughts," I smiled.

"She won't like that, but I appreciate the sentiment." She hung up.

"What now?" Renny asked.

"We need to speak to Rachel somehow. I would also like to know more about Autumn, I can't bring myself to believe that she would poison half a dozen folk around town but she *does* run a bakery so it would be an easy way to distribute it through the food." I realized I was mostly talking to myself, trying to iron out the creases in my plan.

"Well why don't we walk over to the bakery now then, we can grab some food, sneak some my way, and carry on investigating!" he purred.

"Did you hear me? She might be poisoning people through the food, we can't eat any of it. My mom warned me not to touch anything until she got back. I am pretty hungry though...*urgh* but I don't want to die. Let's just go and speak to her, we aren't buying anything."

I heard a low grumble from Renny but ignored it. We couldn't risk becoming the next victims, we had to figure this out and put a stop to the threat. I wriggled my cellphone into the pocket of my jeans and threw the bag onto my back. As we walked down the street, I realized that the elevation of the library meant that you could see the lake over the buildings that bordered it.

I had always loved this view as a kid. The water always looked so still and peaceful, even on days when they had boat races or teenagers doing extreme sports it looked calm. Maybe Rachel had gone to visit the crime scene of her own death. I could try to look for her there after I visited Autumn.

As we walked, I couldn't help but look over to the doctor's office on the other side of the street. How could Dax have come into work today? I felt like that must put a huge target on his back where the police were concerned. The blinds on his window were closed but I could see through the glass door that the receptionist was still dabbing at her eyes with tissues. She seemed more upset about Rachel than her widowed husband did.

When we got to the corner where 'The Twisted Tulip' stood, my heart sank. I had told my mom that everything was fine over the phone, I had been lying that I was there at all. I could now see that things weren't fine; someone had smashed one of the large glass windows at the front. *Darn it.*

"This is a problem," Renny howled.

"Yes, I can see that," I replied. I pressed my palm to the front door and the unlocking process seemed to be quicker this time. I pushed open the door and walked into a sea of broken glass pieces and one lone brick in the middle of the floor in front of me. Who would throw a brick through a window? What if it had hit someone? I supposed I did have the 'closed' sign on the door, it was probably thrown *because* the place was empty.

"Are you going to call your little police friend?" Renny asked.

"I think I'll have to." I pulled out my phone and quickly searched for the number of the station in town. I dialed, waited, and then was pleasantly surprised that Evan had answered the phone.

"Hello Raven Bay PD, how can we help?" he said. I felt myself stand a little taller and then felt silly as he obviously couldn't see me.

"Hey Evan, it's Attie."

"Attie! How are you? What did the rental company say about that taillight I fixed?" *Dang*, I still hadn't returned the rental car. How had I forgotten that?

"Err..." I was stalling as I tried to think of something to say. I caught the brick out of the corner of my eye and remembered why I had called in the first place. "Oh, there has been some damage at my mom's store. Could you come take a look? Someone threw a brick through the window."

"Oh, my goodness! Well stay put, don't touch anything. I'll be two minutes!" he said before hanging up. I was excited to see him, despite the circumstances.

There isn't a lot of traffic in Raven Bay. Everything is so close together that most people just walk from place to place. It meant that with Evan travelling in the police car, he really would be here very quickly. I crouched down to check my reflection in one of the larger glass vases on the ground, smoothing down the fly away hairs and admiring the flame orange color of them as the sunlight shone in through the broken window.

I noticed something else in the reflection, there was something attached to the brick. I turned and spotted a note that was secured with a large rubber band. I knew Evan would be here any second, so I quickly grabbed the note and unfolded it. *'Back off,'* was written in distinctively elaborate cursive. It was almost pretty, apart from the fact it was clearly a threat.

I felt a lump rising up in my throat. This threat was for me. It had to be. I was investigating a mass poisoner and maybe I was getting too close. What was the motive for harming so many people? I just couldn't understand it. Evan cautiously pushed the door open and stepped into the shattered glass sprawled across the ground.

"Attie! Are you okay?!"

"I'm fine. I think the window is done for though," I replied.

"This is unbelievable," he said as he walked over the broken glass. "Who would want to mess up your mom's business? You guys sell flowers, flowers haven't ever harmed anybody!" He smiled at me as he said it, he was trying to be cute. I smiled back but my mind had started exploring. What he had just said was important.

'Flowers haven't ever harmed anybody,' it isn't true, is it? Plenty of poisons are extracted from plants. Could the poison have come from this building?

"I haven't taken the car back," I blurted out. Why did I say that? Renny had walked away to make sure he didn't hurt his feet on the glass, even from a distance I could hear him tutting. Evan didn't seem to notice.

"Attie, won't you get a late return charge?" he asked. He seemed to actually be interested in my wellbeing. He definitely hadn't been into me in high school, it felt like there was a teenage version of myself dancing inside my stomach. "I can get someone else to look into this, why don't I follow you to the return place and drive you back?"

"Okay," I smiled. I could feel my face getting hot under his gaze, but I was so excited about sitting in his car and having some alone time with him. Although as the seconds passed by, I started to wonder what we would talk about, the smile faded as the fear of an awkwardly silent journey dawned on me.

"I'll just make a quick call," he said, stepping back out onto the sidewalk.

"Are you going to inform your mother that her shop is demolished? Or hope she doesn't notice?" Renny meowed from his spot next to the cash register.

"Listen," I said, walking closer so Evan couldn't see me talking to a cat like a weirdo. "I will send her a quick text or something, but it is hardly demolished. We just need to sweep up, get a new giant window and then, what would we do with the brick, dust it for fingerprints?"

"You are asking me like I know," he huffed. I put my elbows on the counter and began to type the message to my mom, hopefully she wouldn't overreact. There was slim chance of me repairing all the damage before she got back from the hospital.

'Mom, big window smashed, glass everywhere, it's sad but fixable. Have to head out to return the rental car, speak soon.' That should do it.

"Hey, could you help me out with something?" Renny asked.

"I'm in a bit of a hurry, but okay. What?"

"Which one of these is coffee?" he said, nodding at two metal tins on the counter. One very clearly had a picture of a coffee bean on it, the other had a picture of some berries.

"This one…" I said. Holding up the coffee tin. "Very clearly. Why?"

"Oh your mom asked me to fill the coffee machine, and I just wanted to make sure I didn't get things mixed up. Every witch in town drinks your mom's coffee, it's a big hit here!"

I looked up and spotted a coffee machine that I hadn't noticed before, it was tucked between the wall and a large display of artificial flowers.

"Wait," I said. "Coffee is made here, and people drink it?"

"Oh yeah, people love it. Witch coffee is delicious, even I like it and I'm more of a cream drinker," he laughed.

My stomach suddenly tied itself in knots and I found myself worried. I didn't even want the thought in my head, but the seed was there now, and I couldn't get it out. My mom's shop might be the perfect place to find a poisonous plant, and if her coffee really was that popular it wouldn't be so hard to contaminate it, on purpose or by accident.

"Did Rachel ever drink here?" I asked.

"Oh, all the time!" Renny grinned, oblivious to my worry and suspicion. Call me paranoid, but I didn't put much faith in the small cat preparing things properly, especially as he had just asked me which tin was for coffee. "Why are you looking all concerned like that?"

"No reason at all," I said as I made to leave.

I needed to find Rachel and ask her if she had drunk here in the past week.

Was there a chance my mom and her bonkers cat had poisoned half the town?

I just had to hope Rachel didn't give me an answer I couldn't handle.

1 0

I fastened my seat belt and triple checked the address of the nearest rental drop off just to make sure that I had given Evan the right instructions. I had never needed a car in the city and I sure wouldn't need one now I was back in the bay. The drive might help me organize some of my thoughts so that I came back to town with an idea of what to do with the notion that my mom might be poisoning everybody in town, even it if was by accident.

I pulled out of the lot behind the flower shop where Evan had thankfully moved my car and began to drive out away from 'The Twisted Tulip' towards the highway. I looked in my rear-view mirror and saw Evan give me a thumbs up, presumably an acknowledgement that he had done a good job with the taillight.

It was a short drive, the radio played songs I had heard a thousand times on my road trip and the local news was focused on advertising a book fair that was taking place at the town library this week. The reporter briefly acknowledged that there had been a recent tragedy but that the event would go ahead as planned.

Was that it? They didn't even say Rachel's name. Was it considered too upsetting for commuters to hear? I felt angry but I knew that it was just misdirected frustration with the web I was tangled in. I pulled into the lot of the car rental drop off and shut off the engine. Evan pulled up behind me.

Something about the police escort made the drop off process seem to go a lot faster. I wondered if they thought I was about to be arrested and they wanted to hurry the criminal off their property. Either way, I was soon sat in the passenger seat of the patrol car with my hands clasped together nervously on my lap.

"Who do you think would be angry at your mom?" Evan asked. I raised an eyebrow at him, then remembered about the brick that had been launched at her business.

"I have no idea," I lied. I knew the brick message was for me. "It's been so long since I've been to the bay, I've missed out on so much change." I was looking out of the window and paying more attention to the buildings on each side of the road than I had been when I was driving myself here yesterday. "When did all this happen? I recognize plenty of people but feel like I just don't know them anymore."

"Does that include me?" he asked.

"I never knew you all that well before I moved away," I laughed.

"Well, I sure hope we get a chance to get to know each other now that you're back," he said. I looked out of the window to hide the size of the grin on my face, he could possibly see me in the wing mirror, but I didn't want to know.

"This thing with Rachel has really made me think. Did I ever really know *her*? I mean, we were best friends for so many years. She could have become something totally different and I'm grieving for a person that didn't exist anymore," I sighed.

"Rachel got married, but you probably knew that already. I figured you would come back to town for the wedding, but you never showed." The tone in his voice made me think he had *wanted* me to be there. How long had he been thinking about me? "That job at the library was great for her, she had been working at the grocery store and it had really gotten her down."

"She had a part time job there before I left, she just stayed there for years?" I asked. I remember her hating it when we were teenagers, I couldn't believe that she would stick with a job that made her so unhappy for so long.

"Yeah, people do weird things. If I'm being honest with you, she seemed kind of stuck in a rut. She married Dax, she switched jobs, she was really making a go of it. She was planning this book event at the library, maybe that's where things got a little sticky."

He had a look on his face that I knew to mean that something wild was flashing through his memory. He looked away from the road for a second to see me staring at the side of his face, it was clear I was waiting for him to keep talking.

"Rachel had big ideas for the place. Good ideas of course, but very ambitious," he began. "The library hasn't had an event like this before, no one knew if it would be a success. She had fancy authors coming to read out excerpts from their latest publication and she wanted to get the place packed full of people.

"She had asked Autumn to cater the thing. You know, put out all sorts of fresh baked goods for people to enjoy during the day as they absorbed the atmosphere. Rachel had thought it was clear that this would be done for free as it would be good advertising for the bakery, Autumn was not sold on the idea."

"They argued?"

"Oh yeah. Rachel got an invoice last week, I think. Well, I was just sat in the corner with a coffee trying to have a calm start to my weekend and she came in waving a piece of paper around and shouting, I was piecing it together from what I could overhear, I wasn't sitting close enough to hear all of it."

I couldn't believe it. Autumn and Rachel had argued, that meant that Autumn would have a motive to cause her harm. But why would she poison everyone else? Had they all offended her?

"That's when Cherry started screaming at them both," he continued.

"Cherry was there?" I asked.

"She is everywhere, I don't know how she does it." *I had an idea about how.* "She was trying to calm them down at first, but then she was shouting louder than anybody. Autumn told them both to leave and they scuttled out of the door. I don't think Cherry paid for her breakfast so that can't have helped things."

There was a knot in my stomach. Two people had publicly fought with Autumn, within a week one was dead and the other was hospitalized. I was putting Autumn back at the top of my list. We were rolling back into town by now and I spotted Gail on the sidewalk.

Evan pushed a button to lower his window and waved enthusiastically at her; she waved back and seemed thrilled to see us both.

"Gail is about the nicest lady you'll ever meet. Present company excluded of course." He was definitely smooth; I'd give him that.

"Hey, could you drop me here?" I asked. He slowed the car down and came to a stop by the door to Autumn's bakery. I needed to ask some questions.

"It's been a pleasure, Astrid," Evan said. It felt like an electric shock to the system to hear him use my full first name instead of 'Attie', I felt like I had learned so much in the past ten minutes that I was swarmed with thoughts, but as I said goodbye to Evan, I suddenly had only one. *I hope I see him again soon.*

I watched intently as the car drove off up the street and turned right on the corner where my mom's flower store stood. It only took five steps to get to the door of the bakery, and once the bell rang to alert them to my entrance, I knew there was no turning back.

How exactly do you hang around in a bakery café without eating or drinking anything? It must make me look like I'm incredibly bored and lonely, desperate to be surrounded by people. I didn't care, I needed to know if Autumn could be the one that was doing all this.

"Attie!" Autumn shouted when she spotted me. She was polishing glasses behind the counter and waved me over to sit in front of her. "How are you sweetheart? I thought of you when they announced that they found Rachel on the shore." She tilted her head sympathetically. She had brought Rachel up before I had chance to.

"I'm working through it," I said. "What with all these poisonings going on, it seems like something serious is taking people down." I studied her face to see if she flinched, if she knew that I was on to her. Nothing.

"Poisonings? What are you talking about?" she laughed. She put down the glass she had just finished cleaning and filled it with lemonade from a jug before handing it to me. I took it and placed it down on the counter, then thanked her despite having no intention to let it touch my lips.

"Cherry collapsed this morning; she's been taken off to hospital and they think she has been poisoned. Maybe food poisoning, maybe something else. My mom's there, the doctor told her that they have about six other cases of it," I explained. I wanted to see if she was getting nervous, but she maintained her look of concern as I spoke.

"Cherry? My word, is she all right? I think the town will riot if anything happens to Cherry?" she gasped, putting her hands on both hips and shaking her head.

"Even you?" I probed. That caught her attention.

"What do you mean? I love Cherry, we all do. For an old lady, she can still party like a twenty-year-old and she is capable of more than any of us could imagine, witch-wise" she announced, astonished that I would question her.

"I heard you had a big fight last week and kicked her out," I said. Autumn pressed her hands against the counter and leaned close, I gulped out of fear. Had I pushed her too far? Maybe I shouldn't accuse a murderous witch of *being* a murderous witch to her face.

"Attie, I don't know what you've heard, but I would never hurt a hair on Cherry's head. That goes for Rachel too. We had a disagreement over the book fair catering, it was a misunderstanding. The kitchen fridges are fully stocked with the food I've prepared for Rachel's event. Cherry and I talked it out and I agreed that working for free, just this once, to help a fellow witch get her event off the ground was worth it."

"Oh," I sighed, disappointed that I had let my imagination get the best of me.

"I haven't poisoned anybody. I run a café for crying out loud, I barely have enough time to sleep, never mind making tainted food for a select few customers!"

"I saw that you took out a book on poison though, a murder book," I explained.

"That? Oh, we have a book club and it was your mother's turn to choose a book. She likes crime novels, you know, hot police officers catching a killer and driving fast cars, solving the puzzles and getting the girl. She chose that book because she thought it was a sexy poison mystery book, she was *very* wrong about that. I loaned it from the library, so did Gail. I wasn't about to waste ten dollars buying it in case it was awful, which it was. I dodged a bullet there," she laughed.

I hadn't looked at the dates when Gail and Autumn had borrowed the book. I probably should have done that before I came in here with a head full of accusations. I looked out of the bakery door and saw Rachel's ghost on the sidewalk.

"I'm a mess, Autumn, I'm so sorry," I muttered.

"You've had a rough re-introduction to your hometown, you can be forgiven for not knowing which way is up," she smiled. I felt even worse about thinking she was a murderer because she was being so kind about it.

"I have to go, I've got stuff to take care of," I said.

"Will you be at Rachel's funeral tomorrow? The poor girl deserves a few friendly faces around her, I assume you have been conversing with her," she said, almost in a whisper.

I was surprised it was happening so soon. I wasn't sure how to feel about it; as she was still able to hang out with me it didn't feel like she was really gone.

"Yeah," I smiled. "It's weird."

"Plenty of weird around here, you'll get used to it."

I walked out of the bakery and the little bell rang as I pulled open the door. Rachel began to walk away from the building, and I followed her in silence in case anyone saw me talking and thought I had lost my mind. She walked across the parking lot at the back and down a gravel covered hill that merged into the shore of the lake. She was guiding me to where she had died.

"Have you figured out what happened to me yet?" she asked.

"No, I have so many questions to ask you first," I began. She sat down on the shore and was staring over at the crime scene tape that was blocking off an area to our left. I sat down next to her and gave her a minute to grieve for herself. "I'm so sorry this happened to you," I said finally.

"It's been a few days now, but each moment there is a new wave of memory about it and I feel astonished that I have left my old life behind. Nothing is the same now. I have sat with Dax in our house and watched him cry, I wish he had the sight like you do. I can't bring him any comfort."

"If we find out who did this to you then I think that will help ease the pain," I explained. "We used to love solving mysteries in high school."

"Yeah but that was always like, 'Who has been putting graffiti up on the outside of the gym' or 'Why are the drama teacher and math teacher arriving in the same car today'?" she laughed. "We only ever really had one proper mystery and we never solved it."

"Huh?" I turned to her; my brows knitted.

"Angelica Burton. Don't you remember? How on earth could you forget that?"

"Rachel, I have no idea what you are talking abou—"

It all hit me at once and I couldn't believe that I had forgotten it either. I started to see everything in my mind as vividly as I had at the time. It had haunted me for so long that I must have pushed it out of my brain completely, but the sound of her name brought it back.

We had been early to gym class; Rachel had needed to run back to her locker for something, so I just walked in on my own. I hit the light switch and saw someone lying on the ground a few feet in front of me. I ran over and saw that it was Angelica, the captain of the cheerleading squad, she was dead.

I had screamed, another teacher ran in to help but she was gone. There was nothing to be done. I had spoken to the police over and over about how I found her, if I'd seen anything suspicious or if I knew of any fights she had been having. She was a popular girl;

gorgeous and athletic. I had been sent to the counselling service by the school and it had helped a little. One day the memory of it just disappeared. I wondered if magic had been involved in my forgetting.

"No one ever figured it out?" I asked Rachel.

"Nope. She was strangled and all the cameras had been switched off for some reason. Plenty of people were interviewed but it just turned into this awful thing that suddenly everyone stopped talking about. I didn't think of it much myself until I died," she explained.

"Do you think someone used magic on us to make us forget?" I asked. "How else could an entire school full of students stop talking about a cheerleader's murder? Maybe the magic stopped working on you after you died."

"Yeah, maybe. Like I said, it's been a weird week," she giggled. "Dying can really mess with your head."

"I believe it," I smiled.

"You said you had questions?" she prompted.

"Yeah, you said that the past week has been hazy, is that still the case?" I asked.

"It's cleared up some, what do you need to know?"

"Did you drink any coffee at The Twisted Tulip?" This wasn't necessarily the most important thing, but I had to rule out my mom as a suspect for my own peace of mind.

"No, I had been trying to organize the book event and your mom offered some flowers to brighten up the library. She was kind enough to bring a book of pictures to me, so I didn't have to leave my office, I haven't been in the flower store for over a month," she said. I felt a sigh of relief escape my lungs. Now at least I didn't have to have the awkward conversation with my mother where I accused her of murder.

"What about Autumn's place?" I asked.

"Yeah, I eat there all the time. Not always a full meal, sometimes I just grab a coffee or a scone and head back to work." *Dang.*

"Is there anything you ate or drank that you don't normally eat? Did anyone cook for you or...I don't know where I'm going with this," I confessed. "I was hoping this would be easier. On TV when they do this type of thing it's always the new restaurant in town or a bitter ex-lover spiking your drinks.

"Uh… I tried a new gin?" she said. "This is a gin town; everyone around here loves it. Loads of folks make their own and try to get it sold at Fives."

"What?"

"That bar loves artisanal stuff; locally produced gin is a big hit. When it gets busy here in the summer there are people making crazy money through their home-made gin," she explained. That could be it! Cherry drank gin at Fives during my party. I hadn't ordered any. I just had to see if the others had drunk it too and… "It's my funeral tomorrow you know."

"I heard," I replied. "Are you going to go?"

"Probably, it's not like I have anything else to do," she laughed. "You have that look on your face like you are thinking a million thoughts, do you need to get back to investigating?"

"Yeah, if it is the gin that is poisoning everybody then I have to put a stop to it," I said, standing up and brushing the dirt off the backs of my legs.

"Then you better go! I'll see you at my funeral, what a weird thing to be looking forward to," she laughed. As before, she faded into nothing and I was now stood alone on the rocky beach looking out across the water. A breeze rolled across and the smell of the lake brought back more memories of the aftermath of Angelica's murder.

Who could have used magic to make us all forget it? I looked at the time and couldn't quite believe how late it was already. The orange of the sky as the sun set was so beautiful. The hours of the day had rushed by me as I ran around town and I hadn't eaten a thing out of fear of being poisoned, my stomach rumbled angrily, and I figured something I prepared for myself at home would be safe.

A soft crunching sound caught my attention. It sounded like a footstep on gravel. The sound happened again, followed quickly by another.

Someone was running.

I turned in time to see a dark, masked figure charging at me. I threw up my hands to protect myself but didn't act fast enough. Something heavy smashed against the side of my head and sent me tumbling back onto the gravel.

The next few seconds were a confusing blur of pain and panic. I had landed on my front and rolled myself over onto my back. There above me I saw the dark silhouette of my attacker standing tall. My vision was blurry, and my ears were ringing.

"Back off!" the attacker commanded. The next thing I heard the sound of gravel shifting as the mystery person ran away from me. I remained still on the beach, staring up at the sky, my head throbbing in pain. This had been my second warning to stop looking for the killer. I feared I wouldn't get a third chance.

My consciousness slipped and I blacked out.

"She's waking up!" I heard a voice shout. My heavy eyelids struggled to open, and when they did, I could see Renny sat beside me on the bed yelling through the open door. I looked around; I was in the apartment above The Twisted Tulip. My mom suddenly appeared in the doorway, framed by bright light behind her that made me think it was morning.

"Attie! Oh, thank goodness you are okay!" she cooed, draping her body over mine like a needy blanket. I smiled as she held me tight and then had a sudden flashback about the event at the beach. "We've been so worried!"

"Who is we?" I asked.

"Autumn found you on the gravel, she called me, and we agreed it was best you come here, and I treat you because a witch mother's magic will cure most things. Just a little concussion really, Dax came and had a look just to be sure, I had already done a lot of the healing by then. Evan came to check on you too, Autumn must have told him about it," she explained.

I blushed at the sound of his name and Renny started purring. "Oh, she *loves* Evan, maybe he is the reason she survived," he chuckled.

"Shush, you," I smirked. My mom beamed at me and stroked the side of my face.

"Do you remember what happened?" she asked. I told her what I could remember. "So, the same person that threw a brick into my flower store did this to my daughter?" I could see her tense as vengeful thoughts swirled around her head. My mom had always been fiercely protective, I wondered what a scorned witch would do in this situation. It was scary.

"I think so. I had been talking to Rachel on the beach and she said she had been drinking a new gin at Fives. I think that it's worth looking into as the source of the poison, Cherry drinks gin too, right?" I asked.

"By the barrel," mom chuckled. "I called her, and she is getting out of the hospital today, she will probably meet us at the funeral. That's today you know."

How could I forget? Memories of a cold case from my high school days were now fighting for priority in my thoughts as I wrestled with the words from the vicious attack by the poisoner. I was getting close. Had they somehow heard my conversation with Rachel? They wouldn't have needed to hear what *she* said to know that I suspected the gin was the source.

I sat up and caught sight of myself in a mirror. "Just so you know," my mom began. "I fixed up the damage and you had a nasty cut, but the bruise is not something I was able to tackle in time. I had to fix the window downstairs and... well long story short, you have a purple forehead." I chuckled at my reflection and saw that my mom had laid out clothes for me to wear to the funeral.

It was time to get ready.

1 2

"We have come together to celebrate the life of Rachel Bailey, a treasured member of our community and a..." the celebrant began. I was distracted by the ghost of Rachel who had been complaining in my ear that she had not wanted to be buried in that dress.

"I just think it makes me look frumpy," she groaned.

"You are dead," I whispered. I didn't want to pull focus from the ceremony, but the sound of my voice had caused a few mourners to turn to see who was talking. I felt like I was getting scolded by a teacher at school for speaking during class. I knew that many of the women at the grave side were witches that knew I could communicate with ghosts, but it didn't negate the fact that I shouldn't be talking at this exact moment.

"I don't know if I can watch," Rachel muttered. "I saw him practicing this last night and it is almost too cringey to look at." The celebrant welcomed Dax to the microphone and invited him to read out a tribute poem he had written himself. "I love him, but this is bad poetry, Attie. I would get out while you still can."

"My Rachel was gorgeous, it's true.

Just three years since we both said 'I do'

69

You fell down on the ground
No pulse could be found,
A part of me died with you, too, " Dax crooned.

Rachel was right, it was atrocious. I lowered my head to hide my smile as Rachel burst out laughing. Dax had picked up the speed to his bizarre rhymes and it felt more like a rap battle than a eulogy. I recognized the faces of most of the people standing around in the graveyard. I saw Rachel's parents sobbing and remembered all the fun trips we had been on together, all the sleepovers I had enjoyed at their house.

"My mom has a Ouija board; we've been talking for days. Dad joined in on a few sessions, but he thinks the whole thing is creepy," Rachel explained. I felt bad that they didn't know she was standing next to me, but Cherry had said they hadn't had a witch with 'the sight' in town for a long time. I was going to be able to give them access to conversations with Rachel that they wouldn't have without me. I felt good about that.

I looked at Cherry who was standing a few feet to my right. She still looked off-color, but she was no longer in pain. She had survived the worst symptoms and come back fighting fit. I wanted to speak to her about her gin consumption, but that would have to wait. Dax's poem ended and he threw a flower onto the coffin in the ground. One by one, the rest of the crowd did too.

I took a rose from the basket that my mom had provided for the service and delicately dropped it down onto the growing pile of stems and petals. "Oh man, this sucks," Rachel groaned. "I didn't expect to *enjoy* my own funeral, but this is a low moment for sure."

I stepped away from the grave and nodded my head in a direction that indicated to Rachel that we were moving away. She followed me across the cemetery to a shady spot beneath a large Cherry Blossom tree. "Is there any way I can spice up the party for you?" I joked.

"Well you look like you headbutted a wall, so that is funny at least. I feel like this town was a safe place to live until you decided to pack up and move back," she laughed. "Then all of a sudden, I'm dead, half a dozen people are in the hospital with poisoning, and you are getting smashed over the head on an empty beach!"

"I don't think it was safe at all," a voice interjected. Standing in front of us was the ghost of Angelica Burton. The cheerleader that died in our high school gym, the ghost that had visited me in the flower shop when I first arrived.

"Hey, Angelica," I said. "Sorry, I didn't see you there."

"No one ever does, you're the only one," she replied. "It feels good to be seen, I've been invisible for so long."

I had moved away shortly after high school graduation. I had left before my powers activated and hadn't been back. I was the only one with the ability to see and speak to ghosts and I wasn't here, Angelica had been wandering around town for years without a friendly face to speak to.

"You all forgot me," she said. "The coven got together to put a spell over the people that were haunted by my death, they wanted you to lessen the pain of my passing so you all had a chance at a normal life. They messed it up though and the effects were too strong. Everyone forgot." So, my mom had done this? She and the other witches had changed our memories so that we could move on? I understood their reasons, but a killer was still free, and Angelica had been alone.

"We are sorry," Rachel offered. "But I'm dead too now, so we can hang out if you like." Angelica smiled softly, it was hardly enough to make up for what had happened, but it was a start.

"I had a funeral and then no one visited me. The spell had kicked in and my grave was ignored," she said, pointing to an area on the other side of the cemetery. I thought about how I wished I had a flower to place in front of her headstone, then suddenly felt the weight of one in my right hand. I looked down and I was holding a blue rose, just as she had asked for when we first me in The Twisted Tulip.

"Why a blue rose?" I asked.

"It's symbolic of a mystery," Angelica explained. "No one solved my murder." Rachel and I followed her across the grass to her burial place. Immediately I could see that something wasn't right. I exchanged looks with Rachel, but Angelica seemed oblivious to our concern.

"What happened here?" I asked.

"What do you mean?" Angelica replied. She was still so young, her ghost forever trapped in her teenage body, adorned with her cheerleader uniform and a look of innocence that had been stolen. I looked at the fresh mound of soil in front of the stone slab that bore her name.

"Your grave looks new, like you had your funeral this week. You were buried years ago, look at the other plots!" We spun around and all the other graves in the area were covered in grass. Angelica's looked newer than the others. "Have you been exhumed?"

"I don't know," she replied, looking suddenly concerned.

"Are you doing okay?" a man's voice from behind asked. I recognized it as Evan before I looked over my shoulder. "Why are you all the way over here?"

When Rachel had died, the spell to make her forget had ended. She told me about Angelica's murder and all the memories came back. Was that the way to get around the spell? Pass on the memory like a torch?

"Do you remember the cheerleader that was strangled in our high school gym?" I asked him. I searched his face for a moment of realization, he gasped like he had just lifted his head up from water after a long period of holding his breath.

"Yeah! Wow, yeah that's crazy. I haven't thought about that in years, how could I forget that? It was the wildest thing that's ever happened in this town." He had the same look on his face that I did when Rachel reminded me yesterday on the lake front.

"Well this is her grave," I pointed out, "and it is freshly disturbed."

"What are you getting at? You got hit pretty hard last night, are you sure you aren't confused?" he suggested.

"Evan, why would a grave be interfered with? Did the police or a judge approve of a cold case murder victim being dug up?"

"Well I certainly didn't, and I haven't heard of anyone else giving permission either. Let me make a few calls." He stepped away and pulled out his phone.

"Jeez, Attie. Stop drooling over him," Rachel teased.

"You like Evan?" Angelica said, grinning with delight that she was able to be involved in gossip again.

"Stop it," I snapped. "He'll think I'm crazy if he sees me talking to you." They didn't care.

"Attie and Evan sitting in a tree," they sang. "K-I-S-S-I-N-G!" They both cackled and, as annoying as they were, I was glad they were enjoying themselves. After several minutes of Evan explaining to various people what he could see at the cemetery, he returned to my side.

"Okay, so it looks like we are going to have a team come over to confirm if this grave has been messed with. If so...well we may exhume the body," he explained. "I said it looks like a fresh grave, so everyone seems pretty sure we will be going ahead. They never caught her killer; I wonder why someone would be messing with her now."

"I don't know," I said. "A lot of strange stuff is going on around here and I need to take more pain meds because my head is throbbing." I tucked my orange hair behind my ears and gently pressed at the bruise on my forehead, as if that would somehow make the pain disappear. Like a child that peels back the band aid to see if the cut has healed after thirty seconds.

"I have some Tylenol in my car," Evan offered.

"Yes please," I smiled. He began to walk across the cemetery towards the parking lot at the edge of the grass and I followed, trying desperately to ignore the kissing noises that my two ghost friends were making at me. "Tylenol..." I whispered to myself. Why was that sticking with me? That word was swirling around my brain. What was it trying to guide me to?

"The chief said that they actually have a forensic anthropologist/author in town for the book fair that Rachel organized. Part of 'her thing' is to offer her help on a cold case apparently, so she is going to head over with the team," Evan said.

"That's good of her," I mumbled. It would be awesome to have a hot shot forensic expert looking at a small-town case like this, maybe she would be able to see something that the police missed at the time. There was no way that Angelica got the full crime scene team that a murder in a big city would have gotten.

Why was I still thinking about Tylenol? We reached the car and Evan grabbed a bottle from his glove compartment. "I just bought this yesterday, still sealed!" he said, handing me the container. That was it! The seal!

"Evan do you know why they started sealing Tylenol? How *all* medication became sealed like this?" I asked. He shook his head. "Drug tampering in the 80's, they had a bunch of capsules laced with cyanide or something. A husband wanted to poison his wife, and make it look random, so he messed with a bunch of bottles in their local store to make it look like a manufacturer default. A bunch of people died. They caught the guy, so obviously his plan wasn't that smart, but I'm thinking we might have a similar situation here. What if something like that happened to Rachel? What if she was the only target and every one that has been poisoned is just collateral damage to make sure the killer gets away with it?"

Evan was staring blankly at me, but I felt sure that I was onto something. What if there was no connection between the poisoner and the other victims? They were all just part of the plan to make it look random. Rachel was the target, she died, the others got lucky by surviving.

13

Evan offered to escort me to the wake that was being hosted at Autumn's bakery. I had taken the Tylenol from his sealed bottle and driven with him from the cemetery into town. The headache was easing off by the time he pulled into the lot and I thought of the book I had taken out of the library; I needed to skim through it at the very least.

"What are you thinking about? Your body is here but your mind is somewhere else," Evan said as he parked.

"I just keep thinking about Rachel and what might have killed her," I mused.

"Today is just for celebrating her life, after the party you can go back to focusing on her death if you want to," he smiled. He reached over and placed a reassuring hand on my knee, just for a second. It was more like a graze than full contact, but I felt tingly. He was right though; I should take an hour off.

We exited the car and walked around the building into Autumn's bakery. There were photographs of Rachel everywhere, a long table of buffet food at the far end of the room and Autumn behind the counter taking more orders. It was standing room only, I wondered if this was because Rachel was so well loved, or people couldn't get enough of Autumn's cooking.

"Attie!" my mom shouted. I stepped away from Evan as she beckoned me over. She was standing beside Cherry who seemed to be wearing an even larger pair of round glasses than usual. "Quiz Cherry, come on! You said you thought you were on to something." I wasn't sure if this was the most appropriate venue for it, but Cherry grabbed me by the arm and we shuffled through the crowd to a back room that said, 'staff only'.

"It's fine, witches can use these places for urgent meetings," Cherry assured me as we sat down. "What have you got?"

"Gin," I said.

"Oh, it's a bit early for me. Just kidding, I'll take a double!" She smiled, leaning forward on her chair.

"No, I don't have any. I'm saying that I think the gin is what poisoned you," I explained.

"You think I drank myself into the hospital, darling, I ain't no pansy!" she trailed off.

"Rachel told me that people make their own gins here and try to sell them on to the owner at Fives. I think someone make a poisonous one. I don't know how gin is made, but that is currently my best guess," I said.

"Astrid Atwood!" my mom gasped. "Botanicals in vodka. It is very simple; how do you not know that?" She looked as though she felt sorry for me, as if gin making was a life skill I should have learned by now.

"What sort of botanicals?" I probed.

"Well you *have* to have Juniper berries, but everything else is up to you. Other berries are probably the most common," Cherry answered. "You get some strange ones, but berries are always a hit with me."

"Mom, do you know any poisonous berries that could have been used?"

"Where do I start?" she chuckled. "The most poisonous would be deadly nightshade obviously. That's the one that's easiest to get hold of. Then you've got—"

"How deadly?" I interrupted.

"A dozen or so berries eaten by mistake could kill an adult. They are very sweet, it's what lures people into eating them," she explained. "It's an important plant in a witch's pharmacopoeia. It was all the rage with medieval witches, I'm not much a of a fan myself. Too risky in my opinion."

"I heard it was the poison Juliet took when she woke to find Romeo dead," Cherry smiled, proud of a high brow literary reference.

"Oh really, well I heard—"

"Guys!" I cut my mom off because I didn't have time to listen to the two of them chatting about Shakespeare. "If someone made a gin with a few deadly nightshade berries then it would get people sick, right?"

"I guess," Cherry said. "Whatever was in there it made my mind all funny. I was hallucinating like you would not believe at your party! At one point I thought the bar had blasted off into space like a rocket, I hid under a table and was shouting and told everyone to strap in. Do you remember?" She was laughing but I couldn't see how a near death experience was so funny.

"I must have left by then," I mumbled. "Do you remember what you were drinking?"

"Darling I couldn't have told you my own name after ten! Sorry!"

"Never mind," I said. I quickly sensed Cherry wasn't going to be much help.

I slipped out of the staff room and back into the main part of the bakery. I caught sight of Owen and it reminded me again that I had a book on poisonings and murder in my bag. Would there be more of a clue there? Or perhaps there was a specific book on deadly nightshade at the library that I could explore.

Dax was loading up a plate with cupcakes and I wondered again if he was the killer. Rachel faded into view beside me and I nodded acknowledgement in her direction. "It's full! I love it," she squealed. "I was worried no one would show up for this bit."

"It's free cake, Rach," I giggled.

"True," she said. Angelica appeared on the other side of me and I was now sandwiched between two ghosts that no one else could see.

Other mourners walked straight through the person they were grieving for, oblivious to her presence.

"Oh, what a sweetheart," Angelica crooned. "Poor guy has had a horrible life."

"Who are you talking about?" I asked quietly.

"Dax. Sweet baby Dax," she replied. I saw Rachel turn and give her a stern look. What was happening? Had Angelica developed a crush on Rachel's husband at some point before she was able to speak to anyone? It felt like a bad time to bring it up.

"He had a good life with me," Rachel asserted.

"I know, but after what happened to me, it's just blow after blow isn't it," Angelica replied, sniffling as if she might cry. Could ghosts cry?

"What are you talking about?" Rachel said, a little more forcefully now.

"Dax and I were together in high school. We kissed once at a party and it went from there. It was a secret though, his dad didn't want him to date and, honestly, I was a bit embarrassed. I know, I know...I'm a terrible person," she groaned. "I was the head of the cheerleading squad, I should be dating an athlete, not the debate club president."

"You were dating when you died?" I asked. Rachel was still displaying fierce body language as though she would need to fight to defend her marriage. Angelica didn't seem to be picking up on it.

"Yeah, my poor love. He lost me and then all these years later, his wife is murdered too. He's the unluckiest man in the world."

I didn't buy it. There was no way Dax had just gotten *this* unlucky twice.

"Did you follow him much, after you died?" I asked. "Who else has he dated?"

"Just Rachel. He was alone for a while, then they found each other," Angelica said, clasping her hands together beneath her chin as though she was about to perform a cheer for their relationship.

Dax had only ever dated two women in town, and both were dead. Both had been murdered. Angelica's was never solved, and then all these years later there was a mystery surrounding Rachel's death that might help the killer get away.

I wandered straight out of the bakery and the ghosts trailed behind as they tried to keep up. "Rachel, did you have any berries the day of your run?" I asked once we were outside. "I know you said you'd had some gin and we talked about feeling strange after that, but what about berries?"

"Berries? No..." she thought. "I mean, I have a smoothie every morning so *that* has all sorts of fruit in it. I buy fresh fruit, divide it up into smoothie bags then freeze it. In the morning I grab a pack from the freezer and blend it up."

"Who has access to your house?" I pushed.

"My whole family," she laughed as though it was obvious. "Dax, of course, his parents, my parents, I think our neighbor has a spare key..."

"I think you were given a stronger dose through a smoothie then," I announced. I was already marching towards The Twisted Tulip. I wanted to grab my bag, then head back up to the library. I could read there, then look for more books to see if anything else had been loaned out.

I hurried across the road, absent of traffic as always, and ran to the door of the flower shop. Using magic to unlock it felt like second nature to me now, I didn't think twice about my palm against the wood and hearing the metal pins turn. I sprinted up the stairs to the apartment, grabbed my backpack and ran back down to the shop floor. Angelica and Rachel had waited for me downstairs.

"I am getting a vibe from you, Attie, a bad one," Rachel mumbled as I locked the store again. "You think Dax did these things don't you?

"Yeah, I think the facts are staring you both in the face and you are choosing to ignore them. You are both clouded with sentimentality for him, I don't have that tarnishing my judgment," I explained.

"There would be no way to prove who killed me now," Angelica lamented. "It's been too long. I'm so sure it wasn't Dax though, why would he want either of us dead?" *Ah.* The motive. That was the missing piece of my puzzle. Why would Dax kill anybody? He had a good career, why would he throw that away?

"Life insurance?" I said, the upward inflection of my voice making it clear that I was guessing. "Did you have a good life insurance policy Rachel?"

"I didn't even have one. What's your next guess?" she grumbled. I could tell she didn't like my train of thought.

"Did you have a lot of credit card debt or something? A gambling problem? Were you a messy person to live with? It could be anything. The motive can come later, I think he did this. I know it's a hard pill to swallow but, guys, you dated a killer." I stopped talking as we walked into the library. Erin was there, working behind the counter this time instead of roaming the floor.

"Erin, good morning," I smiled as I approached her.

"It's afternoon now but thank you. How are you?" Erin asked, giving me the sympathy head tilt again.

"I'm fine, I was hoping to look at a book on Deadly Nightshade poisoning, or something similar to that," I said. She typed into her computer and scanned the search results, typed again and repeated this process until she looked up from the screen to address me.

"I wasn't sure what to look for, so I had to dive into the internet briefly. So, it seems that there are some books on deadly nightshade referenced in one or two gardening books. It is heavily referenced in Greek texts, lots of quotes attributed, such as *'Comes the blind fury that slits the thin spun life'*, which is quite dark." She chuckled. "The poisonous element of the plant, atropine, appears in a medical text and... yeah I think that's all we have."

"Any of those been loaned out recently?" I asked. I maintained my sweet smile, hoping to charm her into giving me information that I probably wasn't allowed to have. She gave me a worried look.

"Attie, I can't really..."

"Erin," I cut her off, hoping to get ahead of her decision to not tell me. "I think that this is what killed Rachel. I think that someone used this poisonous plant to cause harm to all those other people. Cherry was in the hospital because of this, I'm so sure," I pleaded. "Just tell me, did Dr. Bailey take out any of those books?"

Erin began to tremble slightly; I ran my hands through my hair in disbelief. I already knew what she had to say.

"Yes," she confirmed. "Yes, he did. He hasn't returned them yet either."

$\mathcal{E}$rin looked traumatized by the revelation. I had been sitting with the idea for longer, so it didn't feel like much of a surprise to me now. I could see that even Rachel was beginning to believe it, which must be unbelievably hard to accept. Dax was the poisoner.

"Should we tell the coven?" Erin asked.

"I guess, I don't know. I'm *very* new to this," I admitted. "Do you guys not call the police for this type of thing?"

"This hasn't happened before, so I don't know."

"What about Angelica Burton? The coven stepped in on that one quickly, right?" I said. I used an assertive tone, but I felt it was justified. My memory had been tampered with. A group of witches had altered my experience of high school and done the same to everyone else that went there. Who was in charge of the group? Who held them accountable?

Erin slumped onto a stool behind the counter. She snapped her fingers and one appeared behind me so that I could sit down as well. We faced across the library desk like two adversaries about to start taking shots at each other.

"How did you find out?" she whispered.

"Rachel died and I can see her as clearly as I can see you. She remembered it because the spell broke, didn't it?" I chided. I was backing her into a corner, metaphorically speaking, and there was no way to deny what we now remembered.

"You were all devastated. The police had no leads, there was no end in sight for the misery you were all wading through, so we just," she clicked her fingers, "wanted to make things easier. Lessen the suffering. We messed up though, it was too strong, and everyone ended up forgetting."

"I had a million humiliating high school moments that you could have edited from history, but you chose a murder instead? I think Dax killed them both, he was free to kill again after Angelica because he got away with it," I scowled.

"Do you want me to tell the coven or not?" Erin asked.

"Can you make something that can test for atropine? That way I could see if the gin at the bar has been poisoned, it would help do things the right way. I could make something up about the whole thing to Evan and have him send off the one we discover for proper testing; this would just be a quicker way to get to that point."

I was envisioning some brightly colored liquid reaction like a cool chemistry experiment. I would add a drop here and there in different bottles at Fives, find the poisonous drink, give it to Evan and he would find the drinks maker and arrest the killer. Once it was all taken care of, he would take me out to dinner to celebrate being such a great detective team.

"Yes. We can do almost anything," she smiled. "I'll summon the group, meet us in the basement in twenty minutes." She slid off the stool and crouched down. I stood up and leaned over the counter; she had disappeared. There was no hidden trapdoor or a hatch. I didn't know much about magic yet, but that was the most impressive thing I'd ever seen. Despite the circumstances, I couldn't help but be excited that I had so much to learn.

"I can't believe Dax would want me dead. I don't understand, we were so happy, or at least I thought we were," Rachel roared. She was beginning to feel angry, that was one of the stages of grief wasn't it? I couldn't remember the order, or if you progressed through them. I think you just swirled around among the stages until enough time passes and you can move on.

She had lost her life and her relationship with her husband was now over. She thought it had ended because he could no longer see or hear her, but now she knew he had murdered her and tried to cover his tracks by poisoning strangers in town. He was cold, heartless and about to get busted.

"Am I supposed to lock up?" I said to Rachel in uncertainty. Maybe there was someone else here and they had some keys.

"You haven't been to a coven gathering before, have you?" Rachel asked.

"Well a bunch of them stormed the basement after Cherry got taken to hospital, does that count?" I laughed.

"You've asked them to make something, this will be *interesting*," Rachel smirked. Angelica was laughing too, what did they know that I didn't?

As I walked down the hill towards The Twisted Tulip, I caught sight of Dax again. He seemed to be heading into his doctor's office, on the day of his wife's funeral. How could he even think about work right now? He was doing such a poor job of covering his tracks, his behavior was beyond suspicious.

"Dax!" I yelled, causing him to pause with his hand reaching for the handle.

"Hey Attie," he yelled back. I walked quickly to get to the other side of the street and make it clear that I wanted to talk. It wasn't a passing pleasantry, I wanted to search him for even the smallest hint of remorse. "How are you?" He asked once I reached him.

"Not great, it's *just* been Rachel's funeral. It was a sad time, don't you think?" I stressed the word 'just' to see if it occurred to him that his actions were making him look guilty.

"Boy, that bruise is really dark, I should get you something for that. You should come in," he offered. Opening the door of his building and waiting for me to walk inside. I think he knew that I was on to him. Maybe he had heard that Angelica was about to be exhumed and he knew he was on the chopping block once the town found out what a mad man he truly was.

There was no way I would be going into the building with him alone. He would try to kill me, that was his playbook. I stood firm on the sidewalk and shook my head.

"No thanks," I began. "I have some more grieving to do with Rachel's loved ones." He was taken aback at the implication in my voice, that perhaps I was doing *more* grieving than him or that he wasn't grieving properly. I knew he was guilty as sin, so his act was a waste of time.

"I find that any time I start crying, I am completely unable to stop," he confessed. "I felt like things were about to erupt down at Autumn's, so I was just going to lock myself in here and deal with it in private." He rushed inside and locked the door with the key he had been holding the whole time.

"Do you want to miss that ritual, girl?" Rachel reminded me. I didn't know how much time had passed; Erin had told me to get there in twenty minutes. How long ago was that? I ran over the street again and walked through the unlocked door of The Twisted Tulip. I could hear the voices of women, young and old, gathered in the basement below.

When I got down there, the scene was quite different to the one I had walked into the last time the coven gathered. The women were stood, hand in hand with each other, in a large circle around a central fire. They had built a fire on the concrete, indoors. This couldn't be safe. They were wearing cloaks and my mom was throwing fist after fist of chopped plants into the pot that was bubbling on the flames.

"...and wild violet!" mom shouted. A puff of smoke bloomed out from the pot and dispersed itself through the air. I inhaled some as it travelled my way and it tasted like salted caramel ice cream. I had no idea if this was normal witch stuff, but they all seemed to feel comfortable with what was happening. My mom spotted me by the stairs.

"Attie, you missed the good stuff," she sang. She was clearly in a good mood; she always sang her words instead of speaking them when she was happy. "One potion to detect Atropine, an *Atropiña-colada*, if you will." Everyone laughed at her word play and I reluctantly laughed along. I *was* taking it to a bar, it was funny.

"I need to test the drinks at the bar, is this stuff harmful if it is ingested?" I asked. I was worried that I was going to end up either ruining all the stock at the bar or hurting someone else in pursuit of the original poisoner and become a poisoner myself.

"Safe like a bank!" mom howled. They all laughed again; *she was on a roll.* "But seriously, the bar closed for most of the day out of respect for the funeral, it opens again in..." she checked her watch. "You have probably half an hour."

I grabbed the glass container that my mom handed to me. It had a dropper in the lid. "Add one drop and if there is atropine it will glow blue. Have fun!" I ran up the stairs and raced to the street from the inside of the store. I seemed to have lost Angelica at some point, but Rachel was still glued to my shadow.

I could see the bar from the corner and walked quickly up the sidewalk to the front door. I had been running everywhere since I got here, it must look strange to onlookers. I opened the locked door with ease and slinked inside. I could smell liquor, sugar syrups and dish soap, an odd aroma cocktail. I lifted the hatch to walk behind the bar and gazed at the rows upon rows of alcohol on the shelves.

"You think gin, right?" Rachel asked. "This section here is for gin." I stepped over to where she stood and began pulling down the bottles. "They are alphabetical, just so you know. It will help you when you are trying to put these all back."

I worked my way through the gins with 'A' names. *Nothing.* I was beginning to wonder if the potion I had been given would do anything at all. I returned the bottles to the shelf and pulled down a few 'B' gins. The first one, nothing. The second bottle, still colorless. The third...blue glow!

"This is it!" I exclaimed. I span it round to read the full label. '*BB - Bathtub Bounty. This gin is lovingly produced by the Bailey estate.*' "Rachel, does this look familiar?" Her expression dropped as she saw the logo on the bottle. This was the confirmation we needed. I replaced the lid on the gin and returned the others to the shelf. I grabbed the poisoned gin and made my escape, I could give this to Evan, this could be my evidence.

Once I was outside the bar, I pulled out my phone to call Evan, but he was shouting towards me from the end of the street. We walked towards each other until we were within range for a normal volume conversation.

"They are exhuming Angelica, the forensic anthropologist is there now," he informed me.

"Dax killed her," I blurted out. "He killed Rachel too, I'm sure of it. Look, this gin...I think it is poisoned with deadly nightshade. Can you get this tested?"

"Too much information at once, tell me all about it in the car," he said. Angelica reappeared behind him and nodded, she wanted me to go with him.

What were they about to uncover in her grave?

"You think that Dax Bailey has killed two women? I just can't see it, he doesn't seem like he has it in him," Evan mused. We had walked to his patrol car together and were now driving towards the cemetery to, hopefully, unlock the next piece of evidence to lead us to Dax.

I could sense that I was beginning to grow fixated on my theory; I wanted the evidence to point towards the man I suspected was guilty, I should be letting the evidence speak for itself.

"Rachel has a smoothie before her run, right?" I said.

"How could you know that?" he asked, confused. *Dang*, that was information I had gotten from a ghost. I couldn't tell him how I knew it; I would have to lie.

"Err...it's pretty common. We used to do it before we went jogging together at school," I began. "Anyway, I think that Rachel was getting poisoned by the home-made gin for a few days, but he hadn't made it with enough poison to kill her. I suspect that was on purpose. He makes sure a few other people get sick by giving a poisoned bottle to the bar and just waits until people start to get hospitalized, then he is free to give her a higher dose and everyone thinks it's connected to an accidental poisoning."

"Attie, it seems like a stretch," he sighed. "I want to believe you because I know you are doing this with the best of intentions, but it is —what are you holding? Where did you get that from?" I had hidden the gin bottle behind myself and he hadn't noticed it, I placed it down on my lap and he knew what I'd done. "Did you steal that from Fives?"

"Have it tested, if I'm wrong then I'll take the consequences. If I'm right...then you can stop a murderer running free," I pleaded. I had only reconnected with Evan a few days ago, we had spent more time interacting this week than we had at school and I was placing so much faith in him to do this. I saw his face soften, *had I used magic on him somehow?*

"I will test it, Attie. Only because it's you. Please don't put me in a weird situation again though, even a heads up before you do something illegal would be helpful," he warned. I smiled and looked out the window at the approaching graveyard. There were more people than I expected.

"Is this normal?" I asked.

"This is a quiet town. We move at a slow pace out of habit. You brought this disturbed grave to my attention and everyone wanted to get involved as it breaks up the monotony," he laughed. "We had a judge sign off on it in record time, everyone seems to have sprinted here to make sure they don't miss a thing."

We got out of the car and walked towards the sound of the digger removing the top layers of soil, digging deeper and deeper down until a woman yelled, "Stop!" and men with shovels stepped in to do the rest of the digging by hand. To bury something six feet deep must take an enormous amount of effort. I can't imagine that whoever was here messing with Angelica's grave had brought any machinery, so they must have manually dug to her coffin.

The initial excitement of the digger's involvement had given us a false sense of the timeline for the task. I sat in the shade as the sun rose higher and Evan came to sit beside me. He had been to collect a bag from the car and when he returned it seemed that he had packed snacks.

"Weird time to be hungry," I teased. "They are about to lift up the coffin."

"When did you last eat?" he replied. I shrugged in response and he opened multiple Tupperware boxes filled with sandwiches and, what looked like, homemade cupcakes. "I always bring baking into the station; we take turns actually. I think they'll be too busy today to enjoy it, so feel free." He handed me a cupcake that he had decorated with a huge swirl of chocolate frosting.

"You all bake for each other? That is adorable," I said, taking a huge bite.

"We do bake sales for charity, then we decided we should just do it because we enjoy it. I didn't used to cook at all before I became a police officer, they are a good influence," he gestured towards his colleagues standing graveside.

"Is there coffee in this?" I asked through a mouthful of crumbs.

"It brings out the richness of the chocolate," he beamed. My heart pounded in my chest and I felt my crush on Evan jump up a notch to something new. He was making me wish I had never moved away from this town in the first place. I wanted to say something, tell him that he was taking up an increasing amount of space in my brain, but yelling interrupted me.

Evan packed away his last-minute picnic and stuffed the boxes into a rucksack before we marched over to the center of the action. The coffin was now sitting on the side of a giant hole, I wasn't sure if I was ready to see what was inside. I took a step back, feeling suddenly queasy.

I had found Angelica dead in the gym. That memory had been stolen from me and now I was going to see her again, but it would be worse this time. Was I about to pass out in front of all these people? If that was going to happen, I just had to make sure I didn't fall into the pit, that would be embarrassing.

"Are you okay?" Evan asked, concerned. He put an arm around my shoulders, and I leaned into him as the woman that was orchestrating events began to pry open the coffin. She must be the forensic anthropologist that was here to examine the body. This was just work for her, an everyday occurrence that didn't faze her anymore.

"What does it say there?" she barked. "Read me the dates again." An officer close by read out the details from the grave marker and she tutted, then laughed. What could be so funny about a dead teenage girl?

"Ma'am?" Evan pressed.

"This is not Angelica Burton," she stated.

"How can you be so sure?" Evan replied. I had been curled into Evan's embrace, but I peeled myself away to look at the laughing woman in front of us.

"Well this is a man that was at least 80 years old! Angelica Burton is not in this grave. I will need to see records of the plot of land, the paperwork attached with her burial, etc..." she instructed. The officer that had read out the dates from the grave marker pulled out a notepad and began frantically writing down her demands.

"What does this mean?" I stammered.

"I think someone moved her body. I've seen this happen before, a killer realizes that the police are closing in, so starts covering his tracks. *All* of his tracks, no matter how far back they go. Do you have some investigation going on that is potentially related to this murder?" she asked.

"Possibly, it's an avenue we are exploring," Evan replied. "Attie, I will drive you back to town, could you just wait by the car for a few minutes?" I nodded and walked away. Angelica's ghost appeared beside me at some point between the grave and the patrol car.

"They think it's Dax now," she informed me. "Evan is moving towards making an arrest. You did it!"

"Why does it not feel like I did a good thing?" I whimpered. "I thought I would have this nagging sense of doubt lifted from my shoulders, maybe I need to see him in court, convicted of his crimes. That could take years..."

"Talking to yourself? Rarely a good sign," Evan joked as he caught up to me. Angelica blew me a kiss then disappeared once more, leaving Evan and I alone. "I am going to need that gin bottle, did anyone see you take it?"

"The place was empty," I shrugged. "Everyone else was at Rachel's celebration at Autumn's bakery."

"Maybe I can pretend this was left anonymously at the station," he said, taking the gin out of my hands. "They never check the cameras in that place anyway, I'm sure you'll be fine either way." I nervously got into the car; I hadn't even considered that there might be CCTV in there. Would it be stupid of me to try and erase the tapes? Absolutely, I'd never done it before and wouldn't know where to start. Would I let that stop me trying? No.

We drove into town in a weighted silence. Evan was probably thinking about the apprehension of a killer and I was thinking about breaking into the bar for the second time to cover my back in case I had been filmed stealing. Just pile one crime on top of another.

"Stay away from Dax," he said finally. "We have someone coming out to test the bottle, they are driving over from the crime unit in the next town, but Dax will be under observation until then. The thought of him hurting someone else, especially you...I can't let that happen."

"Of course," I agreed. I would be too busy sneaking around the bar to worry about Dax. He slowed down outside The Twisted Tulip and let me out, before speeding away towards the station. I was enthusiastic about the prospect that Rachel would be getting justice soon, Angelica too. I walked into the flower shop and there was a man leaning against the counter.

"Attie, dear, this is..." my mom began.

"You run Fives, right?" I gulped.

"Yeah, my wife is in your coven," he smiled. "Harry's the name. I just figured I would come down to speak to you myself." I felt comforted by his relaxed manner but felt nervous about what he was here to say. I looked at my mom and she took it as a silent request for privacy and scurried away to the rose display.

"How can I help you?" I asked softly.

"I know the coven asked you to investigate the poisoning," he said. "It has hit you all hard and I want to help any way I can. I know you came in earlier and took a bottle of gin, don't worry you aren't in trouble," he smiled, sensing my fear. "I just figured...well if you think it's the gin, you should review the tapes with me."

"What do you mean?"

"I came into the bar one day last week and saw that a few things had been moved around, like someone had come in and nudged things by mistake," he explained. "I didn't think much of it at the time, but do you suppose that it is related to the poison?"

"Maybe, I guess I figured the poison had been added in the process of making it. I think it's Deadly Nightshade berries...we should look at the video," I echoed. I followed Harry out of the store and up towards the bar. As we walked in, his wife waved us through to the surveillance room at the back. I clocked the absence on the shelf where my stolen gin had previously stood.

Harry rewound the camera footage to the night he suspected someone had entered his bar. "I haven't looked myself, it only occurred to me after I spotted the missing gin," he groaned. "I feel bad that I could have stopped this all sooner." He pressed play.

"You couldn't have known," I said flatly. We watched the screen in horror.

We watched the tape back again, then a third time. Someone had taken down at least a dozen gin bottles and added drops of something into each. The bottle I had stolen must have just been the first one, alphabetically, then I had walked away. If I had kept testing them myself then I would have found the others.

"Who is that?" I asked. Harry shook his head.

"It's a little too grainy for my old eyes. I should really update the system, I'm the only one who looks at this footage and I can't see a darn thing," he chuckled. I only knew one thing for certain, it wasn't Dax.

"Can I take this tape?" I asked him. "I need to give it to the police." Harry agreed and ejected it from the machine. It was a VHS cassette, like a 90's throwback movie rental, and I laughed at the thought that up until now he hadn't modernized his security.

I rushed out of the backroom and heard the woman behind the bar mumbling something quietly to herself, speaking louder once she spotted me. "They've got him," she announced. "That wicked doctor has just been dragged away in handcuffs, good riddance if you ask me!"

I continued out onto the sidewalk and Renny was purring by the door. "There you are," he meowed. "I was wondering where you'd gotten too. That weirdo has just been arrested and all is right with the world. Should we grab some dinner?"

"I don't think it was him," I confessed. "I have just spent the past few days determined to prove that Dax did it all, but I was wrong. Harry just showed me footage of some guy, a guy that is definitely not Dax Bailey, adding some mystery substance to a bunch of gin bottles at the bar."

Rachel faded into view before me, looking relieved but angry in equal measure. "What do you mean *you don't think it was him*? My husband has just been arrested on *your* insistence. Evan wouldn't have considered him if it wasn't for you!" she snapped.

"I'm sorry, I just...I thought I was right," I cried, the guilt rising that I had messed about in police business and gotten it wrong.

"You said it has to be someone with access to my house, right?" Rachel pressed. "Let me see the tape."

"Renny, does my mom have a VHS player in the store?" I asked. It was a long shot, but weird things were happening all over the place lately, so I took a chance.

"Ha! Do one legged ducks swim in circles?" he replied. I stared at him blankly. "Of course, that means yes, come on."

In 'The Twisted Tulip' my mom was still faking being busy, I recognized it from my own behavior in several office jobs. Pick up random items and look concerned, as if you are deep in thought and looking for *just* the right item to solve a problem. She had a garden fork in one hand and a helium balloon in the other.

"Mom I need to use your VHS player," I announced.

"Oh goodie, I'll come too," she beamed. She had clearly been bored until my arrival with an unusual request. I followed her down to the basement and she wheeled out a TV on an old metal stand.

"Did you steal this from a school?" I laughed.

"Ask me no questions and I'll tell you no lies. Let's play the tape!" she squealed as I handed her the cassette. She pushed it into the machine and pressed play.

"Rachel is here by the way, I know you can't see or hear her," I informed her.

"Rachel? Tell her I hope she is doing okay, tell her...hmm," she trailed off.

"She can hear you; I don't need to tell her what *you* say," I grinned. My mom was squinting at the screen and over my shoulder, Rachel was doing the same. The grainy footage made it hard for everybody to identify the mystery figure.

"That's my father-in-law," Rachel gasped.

"Is that Bradley Bailey?" my mom asked at the same time.

"Dax's father?" I asked, not knowing the man it was tough to form a frame of reference.

"Yes," they said together.

"Why would Dax's father be doing that?" I asked.

"Maybe to cover up for his son killing me," Rachel whined. "This way no one would suspect the real killer, only you caught him, Attie. He is in jail because of you."

"I guess," I mumbled. "This guy still poisoned a lot of people; he is in trouble too. I will have to take this to the station now." I ejected the tape and climbed the stairs up to the shop floor. Rachel left me to it and Renny said he didn't want to do anymore walking today, so I would be heading there alone.

The evening air was taking a cool turn. The breeze rolling dead leaves along the road was oddly soothing. There were only one or two people on the sidewalk, everyone else in town must be home enjoying their regular lives. The strangeness of my own life had only just begun.

After five or ten minutes I was standing outside the police station, armed with evidence that implicated Dax's father in the crimes but didn't necessarily absolve Dax of them. I stepped through the double doors and Evan was sitting behind the reception desk. It was a small town; he probably wore several hats where this station was concerned.

"Attie! How are you? I'm sure you heard the good news," he smiled. "We made an arrest! He is denying the whole thing of course but..."

"I might have been wrong," I confessed. I slid the tape across the counter and Evan held it up like alien technology. "This tape shows someone else spiking the gin. I showed my mom, she thinks it is Bradley Bailey."

"Dax's dad? Oof, okay," he breathed, unsure of what to do with the information. "Any chance you have footage of him strangling Angelica Burton on this tape too? That would help us out a lot."

"They are in on it together, that's what I think. Dax borrowed books from the library on Deadly Nightshade and poisoning people, then suddenly people are dropping like flies with poisoning symptoms? I know Dax is involved, but now his dad is too," I explained.

"Wait there, Attie," he requested. Evan took the tape and went into the back, presumably to watch it himself. I sat down on one of the plastic chairs in the waiting area and gently ran my fingers over the bruise on my forehead again. The pain was subsiding, but the swelling was flaring up again. I must have looked like a flame-haired unicorn.

A couple burst through the doors and the woman ran to the desk to demand attention. The man trailed behind her, slowly but with an equally sour expression. "My *son* is in there; I demand to speak with him. We have a different lawyer on the way, you can't speak to him without his full legal team present," she barked.

"Ma'am," another officer answered in Evan's absence. "As you were told on the phone, one lawyer is sufficient for an interview at this time. Please." She began speaking at him again quickly, he closed his mouth so that she felt she was being heard, he clearly had a lot more patience than me.

I stared at my shoes for a moment as my brain tried to catch up. If *these were* Dax's parents, then that meant that the man who had broken into the bar was now standing in front of me. Who had attacked me on the beach? Him or Dax? Who had thrown the brick through my mom's window? Him or Dax?

I lifted my head and saw a beastly man staring back at me. He had a weightlifter's physique, he was clearly a man that kept himself in good shape which I would normally be impressed by, were it not for the fear coursing through my veins.

"You must be Astrid." He spoke in a low voice, like a whisper but loud enough for me to hear. I nodded. "So good to have you back in town. Is Raven Bay as you remembered it?"

"J-J-Just a bit more weathered," I replied. What was I talking about? What did that answer even mean? I was just trying to not start shaking in front of the monstrously huge man in front of me, I worried that showing signs of weakness would make things worse.

"Yes, time only ever moves forward," he grinned. Evan leaned out of a room at the back and gestured for me to come through the door and join him. The other officer pressed a buzzer to unlock the staff area and I walked in Evan's direction. Once I was in the room, Evan closed the door.

"I don't think this is enough to go on. It's too grainy, it looks like half the guys in town," he said apologetically. "I'm sorry, I can't base anything on *just* this." I didn't know how to respond to him. I knew he was right, one grainy image of the back of a guy that my *mom and a ghost* identified was going to be hard to sell to a judge.

"Even though he is so muscular?" I tried.

"Ha, we have a lot of weightlifting competitions around here, that describes a lot of the men *and* women in town," he smiled. I knew he wanted to help me, but he still had a procedure to follow. "We will be holding Dax overnight, questioning him and obtaining a search warrant for his house. I am only going to say this once, don't go looking for things yourself, please. It might not be safe."

"I will try my best," I winked. *Did I really just wink at Evan Brooks?* You can't un-wink, so I smiled and backed out of the room. I had an idea that I needed to run past my mom, well I guess I needed input from the whole coven.

I shuffled cautiously past the terrifyingly strong body of Dax's father and stepped out into the cool air of twilight. I tried to think if I recognized his voice from my attack on the beach, but the voice had only spoken two words at me, and it had happened too fast.

I crossed the street on my way back to The Twisted Tulip and thought carefully about how I needed to phrase my query. Some of the urgency felt removed now that Dax was in a cell over night, but if his father was involved as well then I still had work to do. Something about what Bradley Bailey had said brought an idea into my mind and made me question what was possible. Now that magic was a part of my life, I wondered if regular restrictions still applied to me.

My mom was sweeping up when I entered the building. She turned to acknowledge me and saluted in a joking way. "You seem to have helped them catch a killer! Twice! Good work, kiddo!" she cheered.

"Mom, I think it is more complicated than that," I stuttered. I took a deep breath and summoned the courage to ask my silly question. "I need to know more about an event from the past. Is there a way to view it with magic? In my head I am picturing a crystal ball," I laughed.

"Scrying?" she replied, seeming serious. "Well normally we use that for looking into the future, we have some really old ladies in this coven, Attie. If an event of any interest happened in the past then one of them was probably there, we've never needed to try scrying backwards. What did you want to see?"

"I want to see who killed Angelica Burton." My mom tilted her head as she processed my words and I knew that she was unsure. "I know about the spell. I know the coven wiped the crime from our minds."

My mom's face was ashy and gray. "I just...you probably want to know why we didn't do this earlier," she said, her voice shaking. "Attie we haven't talked about it yet. We just wanted to lessen the suffering, but we messed it up. The spell was too strong, and everyone forgot. By the time it was done we couldn't undo things!"

"Mom, It's okay. We have a chance to do the right thing now, and I need your help. So, can we do this?" She nodded. I was going to be involved in real magic, something beyond locking and unlocking doors. Panic and excitement swirled around inside me, but I was ready.

My mom looked at me and could sense my exhaustion. "Attie, these things are usually done at midnight, you can go upstairs, get a little food and take a power nap. I will set everything up down here," she said. It was music to my ears. Renny bounced up the stairs ahead of me and I crawled up on all fours like a toddler; my energy levels were low.

"What are you hoping to see?" Renny asked once I got to the apartment. He nestled himself onto a fluffy cushion that was decorating the sofa and looked comfier than I had ever been.

"I need to know who killed Angelica, I can't get this persistent doubt to ease off and I just need to *know* that we are getting justice for both of these women," I sulked. I had a sudden craving for chocolate fudge cake and knew that I would have the ingredients for it in the house, it was just a case of whether or not I had the patience to wait so long to be eating it.

"You've been here a few days and you are trying to solve every problem at once," Renny pointed out. "I do very little to help anybody and I am happy and relaxed all the time, you should try it." I laughed. It was an enviable existence for sure, but I had known the two people that were now communicating to me from beyond the grave. I couldn't ignore them; I couldn't let it go.

I pulled up a recipe on my phone and set about preparing the kitchen for my evening baking project. I looked at the preparation and cooking times, knowing that the hour required for it would be better spent sleeping. I probably had some instant noodles in a cupboard, I should eat the quickest thing I can find and get into bed.

I found a large ceramic mixing bowl, an electric hand whisk and cake tins. I turned on the oven to pre-heat and then scanned the ingredients list, hoping I wasn't missing anything. I found flour, baking powder and as I pulled open the fridge to grab eggs, I was surprised to see a cake that looked like the photograph attached to the recipe website.

"There is a chocolate fudge cake in here," I announced to the room. Renny leaned from the sofa to look over at me.

"Did you have a craving for it or something?" he asked.

"Yeah, I am literally about to start making one. How...I don't..."

"You're a witch now, it has its advantages. No cake for me thanks, I'm more of a 'beef flavored cat treat' kind of guy," he chuckled. I reached over to turn off the oven and pulled out a plate to carry the giant slice I was about to cut for myself. I would put the other stuff away in a minute, I felt ravenous.

The knife sliced through, leaving beautifully sharp, clean edges to the portion I was taking, and I didn't bother putting the cake back into the fridge, I already knew I would be eating seconds. It was so rich and sweet, it occurred to me that I had only really eaten cake today, again, and my body was likely in desperate need for some nutrients.

I cut the second slice and put the rest of the cake into the fridge. I could eat this, then brush my teeth and go to bed. I would set an alarm to give me time to freshen up before this scrying ritual and then I would be ready for my debut group magic performance. A loud voice inside was demanding a third slice of cake, but I was running out of time to get enough sleep as it was, and I suspected that more sugar would impact my ability to drift off.

I decided to leave the kitchen a mess in favor of going to bed, not the first time I'd made that decision, and Renny joined me as I brushed my teeth.

"What makes you so sure the police can't solve all this on their own?" he yawned.

"They never solved Angelica's murder, Rachel has been dead for almost a week and it seemed that they weren't connecting any dots between her death and the poisonings until I told Evan... I don't know. It seems like I can give them something that they can't get on their own," I explained. I washed my face quickly, changed into my pajamas and climbed into bed. Renny jumped up to sit on the pillow beside me but I was too tired to fight it.

I hadn't questioned why there was a talking cat in my life now. Everything was falling under the umbrella of 'you're a witch', which gave license to strangeness of all kinds. A cake had appeared in my fridge, I was connected to a group of powerful women that seemed to secretly run the town and there was a black cat sitting on my bed that could speak to me. I was about to find out what else Renny could do.

I fell asleep quickly and the dream started almost immediately. I was standing outside my old high school, I looked down to make sure it wasn't a nightmare where I was in front of people in just my under-wear, *no I was fully dressed.* I was wearing the pajamas that I had gone to bed in. I felt acutely aware that I was in a dream. I had heard about lucid dreaming, but this was different.

There was no one else outside, I looked behind me and saw two cars on the lot, but I didn't recognize them. Where was this dream taking me, inside the school? I reached for the handle of the door, but my hand slipped straight through it. Was I a ghost? I looked up at the pane of glass in the door and I had no reflection. Was this a weird ghost/vampire dream?

I walked through the door and tried to push the unsettling feeling aside. I had been through a lot over the last few days and my magic was kicking in, my brain must be trying to unravel the confusion and put things in order. I wouldn't question it. I walked along the corridor and saw the trophy cabinet, I felt pulled towards it and began to read the engraved names on the awards in front of me.

I saw my own name on a trophy for a math competition I had entered. Photographs of my classmates decorated the walls of the corridor, banners congratulating the graduating class hung from the ceiling and... what was that? Someone was shouting, a loud noise followed. It was coming from the gym. I ran towards the gym and saw movement through the small glass window in the door, I remembered my new dream-ability and walked straight through, the two figures didn't notice me enter.

I saw Angelica and the back of someone else. They couldn't see or hear me, but I watched everything.

"I am planning to go to college on a dance scholarship, I *do* have plans," she pleaded.

"What are you planning to study? Dax is going to be a doctor, an academic, an important man in his community," the man barked.

"I want an arts degree, I want to teach," Angelica sobbed. Who was speaking to her like this? The man turned; it was Dax's father. He wasn't as muscular as he had been when I had seen him at the police station. He was younger here.

"Arts degree? Ha!" he scoffed. "You should mix with the people on your course and leave my boy alone. He needs to focus on his education. You are a distraction. A temporary blip in his timeline that could mess up his future. I won't allow it!"

"I care about him...I love him, Sir," she begged. "Please don't stop him seeing me."

"Oh, I don't plan on being the bad guy, not in his eyes," Bradley snarled. "You will disappear, he will grieve and then move on. It will make him tougher; he will rise from this and be better for it."

"D-D-Disappear?" she snuffled.

Bradley pulled a pair of gloves out of his pocket and slipped them onto each hand. Angelica watched on nervously. Out of the corner of my eye, Angelica's ghost appeared.

"I had forgotten all of this," ghost Angelica said. "Mr. Bailey wanted his son to be with a smart girl. He said I wasn't good enough.

He killed me so that his son could get back to his books instead of sneaking out to be with me." We looked on as Dax's father grabbed Angelica by the throat and began to strangle her.

"He killed you because he thought it was the best thing for his son?" I stammered.

"Yeah. He had a PhD in English Literature; he was very proud of it and wanted his son to aim high like that too. He wanted his family legacy to be one of academic achievement, it was his sole focus," the ghost explained.

"A PhD? So that would make him...Dr. Bailey," I realized. Dax wasn't the one who had borrowed all those books from the library, it had been his father. It had been his father the entire time. *He* was the 'Dr. Bailey' and I had pushed Evan towards arresting Dax, when he hadn't done anything wrong. Did that mean that Bradley was the killer?

I looked back over at the body of Angelica, lifeless on the ground. Time seemed to speed up and sunlight crept in through gaps in the door. I watched myself from the past enter the room and discover the crime scene. I woke up in my bed with a start.

"How was that?" my mom asked. I gasped to see her sitting at the foot of the bed. I checked the clock on my nightstand, and it was almost eight in the morning.

"I missed it?" I asked, sitting up in a panic.

"Did you see who killed Angelica?" she replied.

"Yeah."

"Then you didn't miss it. You may have noticed Renny's collar," she said, pointing at the black cat beside me. "He facilitated scrying." I leaned closer to see a small crystal ball around the cat's neck. Well dang. "The rest of us were in the basement orchestrating the magic, but your proximity to Renny allowed it to take place in your mind."

"It was Dax's father. He killed Angelica," I announced. "Is there any way we tell the police though? They will think I'm mad if I tell them *'I time travelled in a dream',* and there wasn't any CCTV."

"We will help him to confess, sweetheart," my mom smiled. "Clearly the poor man is having difficulty with taking responsibility for his actions. A sad story, I'm sure you'll agree." She tucked her long, red-wine hair behind her ears. "It is our duty to help him evolve into an honest man. I think I know just the thing."

She stood and walked out of my bedroom. I followed and Rachel's ghost was waiting in the living room. "Angelica said you know what happened, you saw it," Rachel said. "Can you do that for me?"

"I don't know," I admitted. "I am trying, I promise."

"Are you speaking with Rachel?" mom asked. "Tell her that I will be getting to the bottom of this by hook or by crook."

I believed that she meant it.

1 8

I showered, dried and dressed. It was hard to quiet the voices in my head that were telling me to do something about Bradley Bailey. I had watched him kill Angelica; I knew that he was a murderer but there was currently no way for me to communicate that to the police. I knew that if I told Evan he would only look at me like I had lost my mind.

What if we did manage to convince the police to investigate it, but he wasn't convicted? What was my mom planning to do? I knew that putting my trust in her was sensible, she rarely let me down and she seemed determined to seek out justice, to correct the mistakes of the coven.

I stepped out into the kitchen area of my apartment and gazed out of the window, the lake looked calm and still, the edges lined with optimistic folk hoping to catch fish and for a moment I could trick myself into feeling normal. I remembered Rachel and I sitting on the beach by the lake as teenagers and planning out our whole lives. I had been so ambitious, fearless and driven. Was that still who I was?

"Right," my mom hollered from the door by the stairs. "Renny we need you downstairs. Attie, Evan is here for you." Renny bounded towards her voice and I smoothed down my dress, checked my reflection in the oven door and hurried down to find the handsome police officer that I couldn't stop thinking about. "We will need you downstairs in an hour," my mom instructed. I nodded and she scurried down to the basement.

"Attie, there you are," Evan smiled. He wasn't in his uniform which caught me off guard. "The book fair starts today, and I was hoping we could head over together; I assume you are going." Truthfully, I had completely forgotten about it. He looked nervous as if I was about to turn him down.

"Yeah, that would be perfect," I replied. "I'll just grab my purse. Oh..." I had been planning to run back up the stairs to get my wallet and phone but spotted my purse beneath the cash register desk. My magic must have moved it there. I slipped it over my shoulder, and we walked out onto the street together. The lake air was moving through the town and I felt it sooth me.

"The forensic anthropologist wanted me to thank you," he said. "Apparently this grave situation has been very entertaining for her, she figured out where Angelica was and now the old guy is back in the right place."

"Huh?"

"Whoever moved the coffins just did a straight swap. Angelica was in the grave of the old man. A few graves had been covered in fresh dirt to make it *look* like they had been dug up, but it was just a pile of soil on top of the grass," he explained. "I think the plan is to hold a memorial for Angelica and then bury her again peacefully.

"What about the investigation into who was moving bodies around?" I said, my tone a little harsher than I intended.

"There is a camera facing the access road, we are waiting for the guy who monitors it to hand over the footage. He is a slow mover. He used to work at our school actually," Evan smiled. "He should have retired really, but he loves people watching so much that he figured he should keep making money off it."

We walked into the library and saw the bustle of people inside enjoying the baked goods from Autumn's and the new books that had been sourced for the event. A small stage was set up for authors to read out paragraphs from their books and answer questions from the audience and the forensic anthropologist was standing in the corner of the room doing vocal warmups. I wondered if she was preparing to sing the national anthem.

I wanted everything to be happening much faster with the investigation. I wanted everyone else to feel the same urge to wrap this up quickly. What would the cemetery access road CCTV reveal? Why would someone move Angelica's body? Surely it would be to hide evidence.

I took myself back to the scrying dream. Bradley had wrapped gloved hands around her neck, and she had tried to pry them off her. She had scratched him! In the frenzy of fighting for her life, she had scratched his face with her nails, but it hadn't been enough to stop him. He knew that there might be evidence on her body to lead to her murderer.

I ran over to the forensic anthropologist and tried to get her attention. She was lunge walking up and down the carpet and singing a show tune with her eyes closed. I stood in her path and she lunged right into me and fell sideways. "Questions are for after the reading," she mumbled as she climbed back up onto her feet.

"I'm Attie, I found the disturbed grave that you exhumed," I said, one of my more unusual introductions.

"Ah yes, you were crying at the grave side. We've all been there. I'm Miranda by the way," she shook my hand firmly and then stepped back, stretched her arms out parallel to the ground either side of her torso like a scarecrow and began twisting at the waist. "I do a very thorough warm up," she smiled.

"Would DNA evidence remain under the fingernails of a body for long?" I asked.

"It all depends how long you are talking. Are you referring to this teenage girl we located in the cemetery?" I nodded. "If you assume the police did a good job, then they will have taken samples and stored them properly for assessment once the science existed to do so. Ask your attractive friend over there if they have the samples."

I turned to walk to Evan, it was harder now due to the growing crowd. "Oh, there you are," he said, "I thought you'd ditched me."

"When Angelica was murdered, would they have taken samples from under her fingernails? Would they have kept them?" I blurted out.

"I have no idea, I was at high school *with* you when that happened," he laughed. "I can check. I mean...well we have quite a backlog of cold cases that we just haven't looked into. When I started at the station, they showed me the evidence room and it is pretty huge."

"Can you ask someone to check *now*?" I pushed. He pulled out a cell phone.

"Hey, it's Evan," he said as he walked out to the sidewalk, I followed closely behind. "Can you check the computer and see if we have unprocessed DNA samples from the Angelica Burton murder? There was some suspicious activity at the cemetery and it's making me think we should re-open the investigation. Uh-huh, okay..."

He turned to me and put his hand over the mouthpiece of his cell, "they haven't been entered into the computer, but we haven't digitized everything yet. He's gone to check in the storage area." I shifted my weight from one foot to another anxiously. I heard a muffled voice begin speaking again on the other end of the call. "Great, that's amazing. Can you get that processed?"

I tuned out as they clarified the details of the next steps, but it sounded like they had a sample. Bradley must not have known that samples would have been collected at the time she died. Everyone knows about DNA now; all killers know to try and remove fingerprints or avoid leaving forensic evidence at a crime scene. This is a small town, I doubt that they had the ability to carry out the depth of analysis at the time and unless they had a suspect, they had no DNA to compare it to.

As long as Bradley Bailey wasn't seen by anybody, he would think he was untraceable. For a man that prides himself on his brain, he sure was stupid. He was trying to hide Angelica's body from us in a badly thought out way, he wanted to hide evidence from under her fingernails that the police had been storing all along.

"They can send the sample off to the crime lab in the town over, see if it hits with anything in the database," he said. "They only built that place about five years ago; it's been a blessing."

"I bet," I replied. "What will it take to get a sample from Dax's father to run against the sample underneath Angelica's nails?" I was being assertive because I had *seen* him do it, science was now going to catch him, but they needed a push in the right direction.

"We would need to have reasonable suspicion that it was him," Evan said. "If you are so sure about it, then I guess I can apply more heat to the guy with the security tapes at the cemetery. If we see Mr. Bailey's car driving onto the property, then that might give us enough to request a cheek swab."

"Then let's go," I declared, inviting myself along whether Evan liked it or not. He was in casual clothes, so it wasn't like I looked totally out of place coming with him.

"Okay," he chuckled. He was about to start walking when he turned to me. "Attie, I know you are determined to have someone locked up for Rachel, and now Angelica. It's great to see you pursuing justice so enthusiastically, it would be great to have this much energy at the station. But...are you only spending time with me because of how I can help you with this?"

My mouth fell open. A gust of wind blew up the hill from the lake and my orange hair wrapped around my head like a scarf, I struggled to free myself as Evan watched with amusement. "You think I'm using you?" I finally managed to say. "Evan, I enjoy your company. Let's leave it at that for now."

That seemed to be the answer he was looking for and we began our journey to his car. He didn't have his police vehicle as he was technically off duty, the reminder of it made me feel guilty that I was dragging him back into work. It was a Fiat 500 in silver, a car that seemed ludicrously petite for a man over six feet tall, but he folded his body into it, and I watched in amazement as he did so.

"This is...cute," I smiled as I got into the passenger seat.

"Yeah I get it, I've heard all the jokes, '*you'd have more leg room in a hamster ball*,' or '*does it come in adult size?*'," he smirked.

"No, I like it, not what I pictured you driving that's all."

"It was cheap to buy, cheap to run and I rarely drive far on my days off anyway. It's a practical decision," he explained.

"Then I respect it," I grinned, fighting the urge to poke fun at him. We drove the familiar route back to the cemetery but turned onto the street adjacent to it and up to a house that was living in the shadow of an oak tree in the front yard. Evan killed the engine and we both climbed out of the car, only to find that the owner of the house was standing on his porch, waving us in.

"Officer Brooks, you're back! I've figured it out you know," the old man declared, raising a trembling hand to point at me. "You must be Astrid; he's been talking all about you."

"Can you show us the tape?" Evan said, cutting off the old man. I blushed and I could see that Evan was blushing too, but I pretended not to notice. We followed him into the house and to a room with a series of monitors stacked up. He saw my confusion.

"I also monitor the gym and a shoe store. I just have them recording all day long and if some funny business happens, they call me, and I review the tapes!" he said proudly. "I had to go through quite a lot of footage from the access road to the cemetery, but I think I have what you need."

He pressed play and we watched as a car rolled up to the cemetery gates. Clear as day, Bradley Bailey got out of his car, used a lock pick to open the padlock and then got back into his vehicle to drive through.

"He was in there for hours!" the man informed us.

"Long enough to dig up a couple of graves. This is enough to get the cheek swab from him, Attie," Evan said.

Bingo.

19

———

"Mom, whatever you are planning to do, don't do it!" I pleaded.

Evan had dropped me back at The Twisted Tulip and was taking the tape from the cemetery CCTV to the station. My mom was dressed in all black, her deep red hair braided down her back with daisies woven into it. It wasn't totally weird for her to be dressed like that, but I suspected she was about to do something strange and magical.

"All I was going to do, and you'll agree that it's a good idea, was *record* the scry vision that you had. I would add a charm to Renny's crystal ball collar and wire it up to the VHS player so I could save a copy of it as if it was a CCTV from the time! Then drop it off anonymously at the police station! Problem solved," she announced proudly.

"That has bad idea written all over it," I sulked.

"Yeah, we should ditch the VHS cassette and use a CD or something right?" she offered.

"It's the twenty-first century," Renny yawned. "How about a thumb stick?"

"Yeah!" Mom said enthusiastically.

"Stop. Both of you. There is already footage of him driving into the

112

cemetery at a strange hour. It is enough for Evan to get suspicious and get a DNA sample from him which can then be checked against the DNA under Angelica's fingernails. Let science do its thing, you don't need to involve yourself," I explained.

"Science, pfft!" she scoffed.

"Mom, you are suggesting that you plant evidence, how on earth is that not on the same shaky moral ground as making everyone forget this happened in the first place?" I said. I saw her face drop as the realization that she was maybe not doing the right thing washed over her.

"You have a wise head on your shoulders, Attie. I don't know where you get it from," she smiled. She sank to the ground in a cross-legged position and I sat beside her. The shop floor was wooden and uncomfortable, but she was clearly having a moment. Rachel appeared beside me, sitting in such a way that the three of us formed a triangle, but obviously my mom couldn't see her.

"Rachel is here," I said, gesturing in her general direction. "It looks like Dax's dad is the ultimate bad guy, he spiked the drinks at Fives, killed Angelica and I'm pretty sure he must have slipped more of the poison berries into your smoothie. He could have killed half the town."

"Why would he kill Angelica? I don't understand any of it," Rachel groaned. "He has always been a nice enough guy to me, a little pushy towards Dax, but he wants him to excel. It comes from a place of love."

"I think he thought Angelica was holding him back, that he was neglecting his studies to be with her," I explained. Rachel laughed softly and then her face became very serious.

"He said *I* was holding Dax back because of this library event," she explained. I gave her a puzzled look. "Dax was invited to speak at some huge doctor conference, it would be a great networking event too and I know his dad was keen on him getting a PhD so he thought Dax might meet some research people that could offer him a study program...I got a little lost in it all but that was the gist."

"But he didn't go because of you?" I asked.

"I didn't ask him to, not at all, but Dax suggested he speak at something later in the year instead and support me with this event I'd been planning. It was very sweet and so typical of him to put my needs first, but his dad was pretty angry." Rachel acknowledged that she may have stumbled upon the motive for Bradley's rage.

No one spoke for a moment and my mom, who had only heard one half of the conversation, was sat with her hands clasped on her lap, twirling her thumbs in circles around each other. I filled her in on Rachel's story about the conference.

"He sounds like a parent that is trying to force their child onto the stage, he wants to wear his son like a medal of his own achievement," mom said.

"Yeah, crazy to just decide that he can kill two women so that his son can focus on his work. I hope Evan gets the sample processed quickly and locks him away for a thousand years," I sulked. I was grateful that this was being taken care of by the police, I feared that the coven involving themselves would create more problems than it solved.

"Do you now?" a voice boomed. The bell over the door was still ringing as Bradley Bailey took bold strides into the building towards us. I jumped to my feet and pulled my mom up with me. "What exactly is your role in all this, Astrid?"

"Stay away from my daughter," my mother growled. I was sure I saw a bolt of electricity fizzle across the palm of her left hand, would she use magic against a human? Was that allowed?

"Or what? You'll throw a bucket of orchids at me?" he laughed. His figure seemed more menacing than it had in the police station. I could only assume that he knew the circle was tightening around him.

"I doubt it, they are actually quite expensive," I replied. My trash talk needed some work, but the flash of blue electricity sparked on my mother's hands again and I needed to deescalate the situation. "Why are you here?"

"I have a radio scanner, Attie, that's why I'm here. You've been running all over town with your police friends, dragging them from one breadcrumb to the next until they worked their way to me," he snarled.

"You think they wouldn't have figured anything out without me?" I barked. I was still able to see Rachel's ghost and the sight of my dead friend was refreshing the feelings of anger and my desire for revenge. "You did all this so that your son could be some globally recognized genius, right? Killed his high school girlfriend and then his wife, but you didn't cover your tracks as well as you think."

"Excuse me?" he snapped, stepping closer to me. The blue light from my mother fizzled again and I stepped diagonally forward so that I was between her and the man that was trying to frighten us.

"You think you are so smart, but you forgot that the bar has cameras, you forgot that Angelica scratched you, you didn't think they would take DNA at the time of her death, you moved the coffins and were caught doing it. You painted the target on your own back," I said. I knew that insulting his intelligence would sting more than anything.

"High school girlfriend?" he asked, he face looking a little softer. "What...I don't know what you mean...oh no."

"Oh crumbs. The spell must have worked on him too," my mom explained. "It took the memory of Angelica's death away from all the humans, he doesn't remember killing her."

His eyes darted from side to side as the memories began to flood back, he brought his hands to his cheeks and ran them down towards his jaw. "I killed her too?"

"But you tried to cover your tracks, why move her if you didn't remember it?" I replied.

"I... I thought Dax did it! I didn't want him to be in trouble!"

"You had forgotten, but this is who you are," I explained.

"This Rachel thing, it was bad, I know that, but it was more passive, you know?" he said, looking misty eyed. "I slipped a few berries into her drink and then let the poison do the work for me. I read about it online, I thought if a few people were ill too that no one would look into her death too hard. It worked before...but I guess that was a few decades ago."

"You looked up murder inspiration? It's on record that you borrowed all those poisoning books from the library, there are so many roads leading to you as the killer. I don't know how you didn't see that." It was strange to chastise a man for not covering up his crimes more effectively, but he had left himself wide open to investigation.

"I didn't think anyone would check the books," he sulked. "I didn't think a small town would have cameras in the bar either...I guess I misjudged a lot of things. I can't reconcile with the idea that I have wrapped my hands around that poor girl's neck and... I can't believe I'm that person."

"You thought you were just the, '*murder my daughter-in-law with a fatal dose of atropine*' kind of person?" my mom thundered. "The end result is the same, Brad, women died because you are a selfish maniac who thinks the life of his child is the only one that matters."

"I thought I was doing the right thing, I really did!"

"Have you had a head injury? *The right thing?* You are a murderer!" I shouted. He had stopped stomping towards us to lean against a wall and allowed the memories of his first kill flood his mind. He was clearly over that now and back to his original headspace. "You think you are a good guy, but you obviously came in here to either frighten me or hurt me, so what's it to be?"

The man was delusional, he had actually managed to convince himself that he was justified in his actions because he was trying to help his son get a little bit further up the career ladder. He had murdered two people; I had no reason to think he wouldn't do the same to me if he got the chance. I was lucky to have a card up my sleeve that he seemed oblivious to.

He stepped closer again and reached over to a potted plant that had wooden support stakes plunged into the soil to help the plant grow straight. He yanked out one of the sharp, soil-covered spikes and took another step to us, he was mere feet away from us now. I pushed my mom back as I could see that her need to defend me was clouding her ability to see what was going on.

"Police, drop your weapon!" a man shouted. Officer after officer stormed into the building and formed a semi-circle around Bradley who still had the stake in his hand.

"Put it down, Bradley, now!" Evan yelled. I looked up at Dax's father, the man that killed my high school best friend, the man that strangled Angelica and left her there for me to find when I was too young to cope with it. I was so angry, but I knew that justice here would come in the form of jail time.

I saw Rachel rush towards Bradley, what was she about to do? As her ghost form hit him, he clearly felt something. Maybe it was a cold chill or fear, but he leapt up into the air like a cartoon cat that saw a dog. This caused the police to fire tasers at him and it seemed that prongs hit him from all sides. He landed onto the ground with a thud and my mom wrapped her arms around me from behind, squeezing me so tightly I couldn't take a deep breath.

I watched Evan kneel down beside the giant man, securing handcuffs around his wrists, before the other officers pulled the arrestee up to his feet and escorted him out of the door. I couldn't see Rachel anywhere. Evan ran towards me. "Did he hurt you?" he asked, slightly breathless from the frantic activity of the last few minutes. I shook my head. He ran out after the other officers and then my mom and I were alone.

It was done.

2 0

"*H*ow many of those have you had?" Evan asked. I was just polishing off my third Caffe mocha as Evan arrived for our lunch date. No one had *technically* used the word 'date', so *technically* we were just meeting up for a bite to eat, but I was hoping it would blossom into something more.

"Never you mind what she's been doing while she was waiting for you," Autumn barked from behind the counter. "What time do you call this?"

"I... there's been a lot at work, I had to finish off some admin before I could leave," he stammered. It was funny to watch how quickly Autumn could tear down the bravest of men when they came into her bakery.

"I've not been here all that long," I lied. "Is it bad over there?" It had been over a week since Bradley's DNA results had come back as a match against the sample taken from Angelica's fingernails. Dax had been released and had obviously been struggling to come to terms with the fact that his father had killed for him twice and hidden it.

"There have been a few complaints about the Fives party, and by 'a few complaints', I mean that I have had one very angry lady on the phone three times a day," he complained.

118

It had been decided that, after all of the gin in stock at Fives had been discarded, that a 'The gin is back' party should be organized and would be used as a joint celebration to honor Rachel and Abigail also.

I tucked a strand of my ginger hair behind my ears to get it away from my face as Autumn placed an orange roll down in front of each of us. "Thanks," I smiled. She winked as she walked away, I had no idea what the winking was referring to, but I felt myself blushing under her gaze. It felt like being on a date with a parent sat one table over.

"So, what's next Officer Brooks? Will you be drinking the gin of the townspeople tonight?" I asked. There had been a rush for gin making supplies as everyone wanted a chance to have their home-made drinks stocked on the shelves. My mom and Cherry had been working on a few flavor combinations and all of them were glowing in neon colors. I suspected that they tasted amazing; I hadn't been allowed to sample any yet.

"I'll be there if you will," he grinned. "Sorry that was embarrassing. I'm no good at this."

"No good at what?"

"Flirting," he blushed. I bit my lip as this was as good as verbal confirmation that we *were* on a date.

"You are better than you think you are. You saved me from getting murdered less than seven days ago, don't forget! I was *really* into that," I joked. He laughed with me and we ate our pastries under Autumn's watchful eye. I wondered if she was required to report back to my mom afterwards. I was an adult now though, it was crazy. They all treated us as if we were still in high school.

"True. Although in that situation I guess I also saved your mom's life and I haven't taken her out for lunch," he teased. I couldn't tell him that I never had any doubt that my mom would have blown Bradley into a thousand pieces with her magic if we had been alone with him. She was never in any danger.

"How have the nightmares been?" he asked. I looked down to avoid my eye contact with him. I had been having anxiety dreams since Bradley was dragged out of the store. I was reliving the attack on the beach, reliving the discovery of Angelica in the school gym...but not last night. Last night was a good dream, Evan and I alone on a boat on the still lake water.

"They seem to be easing off," I said. "Putting more time between me and this whole mess will probably be enough to bring back happier thoughts."

"You went through something traumatic, you should speak to someone," he said. He reached across the table and placed his hand on mine, just for a second. I looked down to see where his skin was touching me and saw a small shot of blue electricity across my hand. I quickly made a fist to hide it from him. We had touched and there had literally been sparks, I would have to tell Rachel when I next saw her.

Out of the window I could see my mom and Cherry hauling a wooden barrel of something along the sidewalk in the direction of The Twisted Tulip. Someone should probably warn the bar patrons about their gin later. Evan was still waiting for a response.

"Yeah, yeah I will," I said. I wondered if there was a special witch therapist I could speak to. I had lived my life as a regular, human girl and then moved away from town at a critical age which meant that I had missed out on so much. Raven Bay was a mystical place and I had only cleaned up one ongoing mystery that had been hanging over this town.

The flawed spell that the coven had placed over us to lessen the grief of Angelica's murder seemed to have accidentally erased other memories as well. They were coming back to the affected recipients in small doses and not all at the same time, but I was beginning to remember strange conversations with my grandmother that had happened before she died.

I didn't know if I should speak to my mother about it yet or not, I wanted to see what else I could remember first. I had worries that the coven was hiding things from me, but I couldn't say it to anyone. Not yet.

Evan's phone started to ring, and he put down the menu he was reading and went to answer the call. After a short conversation it was clear that he was needed back at the station.

"I'm so sorry, there's a small fire in the break room and apparently that means I need to go back. I'll see you tonight, I promise." He apologized again, left money for whatever it was that I wanted to eat and ran for the door.

"Oh, real great start to this relationship huh? What a dingus!" Autumn yelled after him. Her daughter joined in jeering at Evan's back as he jogged away up the street. I laughed at the pair of them and requested soup and a roll, hoping my order would distract them from making fun of a man that was into me. It felt strange to even think it after all the dizzy daydreams I'd had about him in high school, but Evan Brooks was definitely into me.

"Thank goodness he's gone," a woman whispered to me. Sitting across the table from me was the ghost of my deceased grandmother. I knew that this meant no one else could see her, so any conversation from me would make me look like I was talking to myself. "I've been trying to get your attention since you arrived in this town but you sure are a busy gal and I don't move all that fast."

"Long time no see," I whispered back. "I'm still new to all this."

"Yes, I know. You never should have left, but that's another story for another time," she began. "Now that you have finished messing around with random ghosts, are you going to clean up this place?"

"What do you mean?" I asked, pretending to read the menu again in case anyone was watching.

"You moving away put things out of balance, sweetheart. I would have stopped you but I was obviously dead by then and there is a *chance* that I forgot to mention to anybody that the balance of good and evil magic is something to keep an eye on around here. I was going to tell your mother once, but then I forgot!" she shrugged.

"Balance?"

"Well you are a good one, look at those big beautiful eyes of yours, you're a flame haired angel," she swooned. "But there is bad magic too. When you left there was no longer an equal amount of good energy to counter the bad. There is a lot going on around here that you need to fix, baby girl."

She vanished into thin air as Autumn brought over my soup. My grandmother didn't reappear during lunch, or at any point during the afternoon back at The Twisted Tulip when my mom and Cherry were decanting their gin into various glass containers.

I went up to my apartment and could hear a lot of loud voices coming from inside. I recognized Renny's voice among the shouting but couldn't imagine what was going on behind the door. All I wanted to do was put on some make up, curl my hair and throw on a cute dress before going on another date with the handsome police officer of my dreams.

I unlocked the door and silence fell over the people inside. I let out a long exhale and hung my head as I pushed the door closed behind me. I didn't know a single one of them. Granny emerged from the group and that's when I realized they were all ghosts.

My sight had grown stronger in the few days I had been here, and ghosts were now appearing to me as solid and real as any living body. My apartment was filled with the dead. "Thank goodness you're here!" Renny moaned. "They have a lot to say and I'm not really a problem solver."

Problems?

"This is my granddaughter, Astrid. She can help us!" granny told them. A few weeks ago, I had been struggling to figure out what I was supposed to do with my life. I guess now I had found my purpose.

"Okay, who's first?" I asked.

THANKS FOR READING

Thanks for reading, I hope you enjoyed the book.

It would really help me out if you could leave an honest review with your thoughts and rating on Amazon. Every bit of feedback helps!

Book 2 coming soon! x

MAILING LIST

Want to be notified when I release my latest book? Join my mailing list. It's for new releases only. No spam.

http://eepurl.com/gIHYJj

www.ingramcontent.com/pod-product-compliance
Lightning Source LLC
Chambersburg PA
CBHW022007170726
47994CB00023B/2408